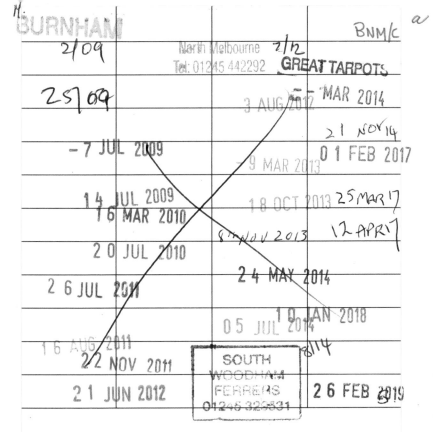

This book is to be returned on or before the date above.
It may be borrowed for a further period if not in demand.

Essex County Council

SILVER STREET

Iris Black falls for Johnny Fenwick, but decides she wants more from life than becoming his wife, and goes to train as a nurse. The Second World War is looming and she is determined to do her part. At the front line she learns to survive, to put the patient first, and to fight tiredness and despair – and she also learns about love. Johnny is still suffering from her rejection when he meets Nan Fielding, a shy, impoverished girl who no one bothers to get to know – but will Johnny be able to forget about Iris, the girl who left him behind?

SILVER STREET

SILVER STREET

by

Elizabeth Gill

Magna Large Print Books
Long Preston, North Yorkshire,
BD23 4ND, England.

British Library Cataloguing in Publication Data.

Gill, Elizabeth
    Silver Street.

    A catalogue record of this book is
    available from the British Library

    ISBN   978-0-7505-2908-2

First published in Great Britain in 2008 by
Severn House Publishers Ltd.

Copyright © 2008 by Elizabeth Gill

Cover illustration © Rod Ashford

The moral right of the author has been asserted

Published in Large Print 2008 by arrangement with
Severn House Publishers

Magna Large Print is an imprint of Library Magna Books Ltd.

Printed and bound in Great Britain by
T.J. (International) Ltd., Cornwall, PL28 8RW

This story came out of the early life of my aunt, Janet Gill, who was a nurse in the Second World War, and came home to face the single life in Durham. I hold dear the little circle of gold on a man's watch chain. All it says is 'In memory of Johnny'.

Prologue

Johnny Fenwick. Iris would lie under the blackness of the Egyptian night and say his name beneath her breath. Somehow she thought if she could say it often enough she could make him real, make him hers once again. She could not bear the idea that he never would be hers. Around her wrist she wore the bracelet he had had fashioned for her from a watch chain. It was heavy because she had slim light wrists but for a watch chain she supposed it was thin and light. On it was the little gold disc which read 'In memory of Johnny'. She would never take it off, nor cease to think about him.

It was time to leave this place and go home. The war was over. She had been at Dunkirk, then Egypt and finally back to France again for the end and she must go back to what she had before, to whatever was left in the little northern city which she had thought she loved so much. She dreaded it. Everything had changed, everywhere had altered and she knew enough of life now to understand that the reverberations of war fell even in Durham, where every family had lost somebody, the big munitions factory at

Aycliffe had been a big women's contribution to the war effort and every second person you saw was in uniform of some sort. It was finished, she could not believe it.

She had no heart to go home but there seemed nowhere else to go, nothing to do. Strange that the freedom should feel like a trap and Johnny would not be there.

She stood on King's Cross station, remembering the time when she had come back from Dunkirk and seen him on the platform, and she could not help looking among the tall dark figures and imagining that he would emerge, that she would recognize him and every time she looked the man was shorter or taller, thinner or wider, did not have Johnny's gait nor his hair colour, nor that indefinable something which made each person unique.

She knew that she would not see him again this side of whatever heaven there was. Yet she could not help but look endlessly into the crowd and wait and hope and imagine that he must be there somehow, some time, in some place where everybody met again.

King's Cross was the loneliest place in the world, she thought, with lovers rushing into one another's arms, families standing together, soldiers in groups, pigeons picking up crumbs from the ground, the odd sparrow lost. That was how she felt, alone and lost in

this great booming space when everybody had somebody except the drunks.

One of them approached her, his breath stinking of sherry, his clothes shiny with use and grime and an Irish accent on his lips. He had piercing blue eyes for all they were glazed over and she wondered what dreadful things had befallen him so that he could no longer face his life sober and he begged her for a few coins with a sweet smile and told her she was the most beautiful woman on earth and she laughed and said, 'You haven't seen many then,' and she reached into her pocket and gave them to him.

She didn't care that he should spend it on drink, she hoped he would if he could not get by without it. Who could get by without something to help? Who could look into the light of day and not wish things otherwise? God damn it, she thought, angrily, it was hopeless.

You're tired, she told herself, too tired and making too much of everything. You'll be all right when you get home.

'Got a light, love?'

She turned as the man behind her looked hopefully towards her. He was a soldier, not a drunk, not somebody desperate for any-thing except the sweet pull of a cigarette and he had the cigarette, he only needed a match. His eyes were the same blue as Johnny's eyes

had been but of course he was not Johnny. As she hesitated he smiled at her. He was young. Was he going home to somebody he loved? She hoped so. He looked weary but he had made it through. She wanted to cheer.

'No, no, I'm sorry. I wish I had.'

He looked surprised but offered her a cigarette which she took and then he moved off, cigarette between brown, stained fingers. She was now desperate herself for the cigarette and in turn asked another soldier, standing nearby, for a light and she stood there, taking the smoke into her lungs and was aware of letting go of her breath, relaxing finally as she waited.

The train was ready now and she made her way gratefully towards it, wanting nothing but to see familiar places, and her family, to see what there was to go forward to, what there was if anything left to go back to. It was a strange world without war, and rather frightening.

She could not think what she would do with the rest of her life but she felt – and it was trite she knew – that she owed it to all those people who had died to get on with it, to try to make something good from it.

The train was packed, there was nowhere to sit. In the end she stood her suitcase on end and perched on that while the rain settled in and the light faded.

The train made its comforting rhythmic noise northward, first Stevenage, then Peterborough and Doncaster, she knew it so well and she would have given a lot to be able to see the countryside. She almost fell asleep twice but was in danger of falling off her suitcase and so on to the floor.

York was difficult because she and Johnny had spent their last night in York. She breathed carefully as the train stopped. Although she wanted to get out and run up the platform, almost certain that he would be with her, she knew in her heart that he was not. She made herself stay on the train until thankfully it pulled away and she knew that it would not be long now, less than an hour until she got home. Eventually they pulled into Darlington station and there her courage once more came to her aid. Fifteen minutes.

Durham station was next and surely her brother, David, would have come to meet her and once she was home ... it was all she could think about, being home, lying in a soft bed. Did she remember what a soft bed felt like?

She was not sure. She did not feel entitled to such things, she could not help the guilt she felt, that she was alive when so many had died, so many nurses had, doing brave things such as she thought she never could have, shielding their patients from bombs, from aircraft fire. So many of them would not come back. She was lucky. She didn't feel lucky, the whole idea made her shiver.

When the train finally stopped at Durham everything seemed to be in darkness and she struggled with her luggage. Behind her back as she stood on the station somebody said her name and in some stupid wildness, hearing the sweet flat northern accent, she turned with the joy of Johnny's name on her lips.

She was able to stay the noise before it left her, to halt her breath. The man behind her was her beloved brother and she felt the tears which she had held off for so long and she held them back now so that he should not feel uncomfortable or embarrassed.

'David,' she said, 'how lovely to see you.'

It was not true. She couldn't see him at all, she couldn't see anything, not even her parents who had come forward to embrace her. The world was another place and she was like somebody from a different planet.

'It's all right,' he said, 'you're home now.'

It was not true of course, nothing was all right and never would be. And she would not forget the men she had nursed, those who had died, those who were so badly injured that their lives were changed, the friends who would not be coming home.

There was nothing left to come back to somehow. She was numb. She wished that she had never gone, that she could have been like so many women, married, had children, been stuck here with the domestic trivia, the day-to-day problems of putting food on the table and keeping things going.

She could have been safe in that stupid castle which Johnny called home. Why had things worked out like they did, why had she let life take her rather than she it, and then she thought, I did, I took charge and if it wasn't what I wanted then at least I had my choice and if it was wrong then it was and I must take responsibility for that.

David drove the car through the familiar streets, down the winding bank which led from the station into North Road and then into the narrow streets of the city and she recognized them and she wound down the window to smell the river. The Wear smelled like nothing else, warm and muddy and of recent rain, and she remembered that from her window on a summer's night she could hear it making its way to the sea or could she?

Did her memories play her false and was it just that she imagined she could hear the water make its gushing way past the cathedral and the castle and the loop around the city when the rains had been heavy and it was brown and white with froth? And in the summer when the river was low and it slid over the big flat green stones which had been there for so long could she hear it

17

then, so soft in its journey to Sunderland?

The streets were small. She had forgotten how perfect the city was. The tall narrow buildings, the round polished cobbles shiny because it had just rained, the tiny windows, the Durham bays which were upstairs and somehow the downstairs rooms did not have them, they jutted strangely and beautifully, she thought.

The shops were closed, the pavements deserted, it was growing late. She had dreamed so many times of coming home and her heart twisted because just for once it was everything and more than she had thought it would be. She had travelled thousands of miles and experienced things which few women from Durham had known before and all she wanted now was some peace.

Finally David halted the car before the house and this was something else which she had dreamed of. Had her home always been so big, looked so welcoming? The solid square stone house where she had been born was as much as any woman could imagine.

The lights with the curtains drawn back, perhaps for her homecoming, spilled out cream on to the driveway. She had not seen it like that in years, before the blackout.

She had thought so many times that she would not come back here, that she would be killed and she would not feel the comfort of her parents' bodies against her, her father

smelling of tobacco and the foundry somehow, the dust and the grime, her mother of
perfume and gin on her mouth as she kissed
Iris once more.

It smelled like home, the wood smoke
from the chimneys, the mint wet with dew
beside the back wall, the lavender along the
path which in August would brush its scent
against her legs.

Going inside was so alien. Had this really
been her home, the smell of polish, coffee,
cake, good cooking – some kind of stew?
Music was playing on the radiogram, her
father's favourite, Chopin's nocturnes.

The rooms were softly lit against the
shabby furniture, the old leather chairs with
their all-compassing arms, the big fire in the
old marble fireplace. Her mother gave her
tea and scones, butter and raspberry jam.

Time had altered. That first evening
crawled past, there was nobody to look
after, no friends to talk to. She wanted to
excuse herself and go to bed and yet her
parents looked at her as though they were
amazed she had come back to them, they
could not quite believe it and she did not
want to disillusion them with tears or sleep
or resignation or dreadful stories and so
there was nothing to say. All she had to do
was get through the evening.

She had thought she wanted to unburden
herself but she couldn't. They would not

understand how she felt, what she had seen, what she had endured and their lives were so different. Having wanted to be home so much she felt that she could not rest.

It was only later, when her parents went to bed and she and David were left, she curled up in the cushions of the sofa and he gave her a huge glass of whisky, that she felt her body relax.

'What happened to Johnny?' David said. 'You never said.'

She did not tell him. She told him what she thought he could bear, what she knew he could stand. She did not tell him how afraid she had been, how she had contained her fears, taught, she knew now, by those impossible people at the Royal Victoria Infirmary in those far-off days of her training in Newcastle.

They had taught her endurance, how to survive, how to put the patient first, how to contain her own feelings endlessly, how to fight tiredness and despair. They had not taught her what to do when everything in her life seemed over. She would have to learn that for herself. She had a feeling that it would be just as difficult in its way as the war had been and she would have to do it alone.

Her bed, when she finally got there – she was hazy with drink – was too soft, too big. Her room was enormous. She threw back the curtains and there was the North Star. It made her weep such as it never had before. She could feel the tears running down her cold thin cheeks. She had not cried in France or in Egypt. There she could not let go. Now she had no reason to hold back any further.

How could it still be there after so many people had been injured and died, after men had lost their wives and children, their independence, their minds? How could it still go on? And she was so glad to see it. It was the star that she and David had watched from their bedroom window when they were children, when they walked up Silver Street towards home on frosty December nights and moonlight made the cobbles glisten like pearls, it was always there.

She loved Durham. Of all the places she had been she loved this one best. It was such a glorious tatty little town, with its magnificent buildings, dirty streets and winding grey river. She was finally pleased to be home. She swore she would never ever leave it again. The star on Silver Street shone and it was still hers. It always would be.

One

One of Iris's favourite memories of childhood was herself and her young brother, David, lying in the big back bedroom at home watching the cars come down the hill in the darkness.

In her best dreams she and David were sitting there, nobody else anywhere around, the whole world packed up and gone away. He was a very little boy and she was his big sister and he was maybe four and she was maybe nine and the bed was feathers, soft and thick and it was enormous, even with two of them sitting there.

In the darkness when their parents had gone downstairs, in the quietness beyond the hills of Durham, there was nothing to see but the black sky and the lights of cars as they came over the top of the hill and were about to descend into the sleeping town, and they would sit there, propped with pillows and talk. She could not remember what they talked about; it was never of any consequence, it was always just that wonderful comfortable stuff people talked about when they knew one another well.

In later times of her life, when things got

too bad, Iris imagined the nights of her childhood, the feeling secure which you never did again, knowing that her mother and father were sitting over the fire downstairs and there was nothing beyond the house which mattered, she imagined the quietness of the shops being shut and the people huddled in their houses against the cold northern wind and the rain. She kept the image close when there was nothing else to keep close in the cold desert nights with the sound of the hurt and the dying never far away. During those times, when she was not on duty, when she was trying to sleep, she imagined the life which they had led when she was a child and before everything had gone wrong.

David, from the beginning, was a nice little boy. She resented him terribly at times because she had been the first child and for some reason, because he was a boy, people were so very pleased when he was born and she was all set to hate him but he was difficult to hate. She would instigate plans and David would help her put them into action.

They led a free life. Even on Sundays when other children were dragged to Sunday school somehow they managed to get out of it and pull on old clothes and, as far as their parents were concerned, disappear for the entire day and nobody ever suggested to them that they should stay near or that they should not go to their favourite places.

They would walk miles to play on certain swings. They had an old tent which they would pitch as far from the house as they could and build a fire and take a milk pan which their mother had given them and cook on it various fruit and vegetables from the garden. Their favourite was rhubarb. They would camp out overnight there with friends and build a bonfire and cook potatoes in the embers. They would play soldiers or hide and seek on the railway and in the fields and on the pit-heaps which lay beyond the town. Many of the pits were closed or closing but there were lots of little pit villages for miles beyond the city.

Iris, David and their friends would play noisy games, screaming and shouting. From time to time people complained, so her mother said, that the Black children were running wild and shouldn't they be controlled more. Iris was half convinced her mother made this up from a sense of mischief but if people did say they should be sitting in church learning about the parables (they had lots of books at home and Iris knew the parables almost by heart so she couldn't see the sense to it anyway) then they were wise enough not to burden Iris and David about it.

Perhaps it had something to do with the fact that their grandfather had been a

Methodist minister. Iris didn't remember him well, just that he was very good at playing the piano and that he and her mother would talk about David's future and wonder if he couldn't make the Church part of his life.

She had the feeling as she grew older that they were humouring one another and no more, in the deluded way that people did, with the idea that it was something the other person really wanted. Whatever, David was never the kind of boy who would have been an asset to the Church.

What he really loved was the sea. It was hard work going anywhere near the coast with David because he could spend hours among the trawlers at Whitby and was always desperate to see how the ships were built on the Tyne. Her most enduring memory of him as a child was making harbours in the stream below the house by moving stones around, and building boats and sailing them and of her mother's perpetual worry that he would fall in and drown.

When they went on holiday it was always to the seaside and if you weren't careful you virtually lost David there for a week or a fortnight or however long it was because he was always on the beach watching people fish, or at the end of the pier catching small crabs, or taking a bucket to the rocks and putting hermit crabs inside so that he could watch them carrying their homes around for a while before kindly putting them back into the pool from where they had come.

She built sandcastles and she could remember him going down to the sea to fetch blue bucketfuls of water back for the moat. He was a tubby little boy with short legs and had sandy hair which blew in the breeze which inevitably got up either on the shore or off it this far north.

She would dress her sandcastles with flowers from the dunes, pink and blue, and David would dig the moat and fill it with water and when the tide came in they would watch the waves break upon their sandcastles and drag the sand back into the water with foam and bubbles. She loved the way that the tide went up and down twice a day and renewed the beach like an empty page so that you could begin again the next day.

They went looking for shells and she made trinket boxes and stuck on them her very best finds and sometimes there was sea coal on the shore and strange rocks like jewels and now and then jellyfish brought in on the last tide, see-through, with intricate purple middles like the tops of violet creams.

There were starfish in the pools and sea urchins, and people caught crabs and cooked them on Primus stoves, and winkles which you had to prise out of the shells with a pin.

As the children got older their father took them to the seaside almost every weekend in the summer where they hired a place at a little village in Northumberland called Alnmouth. Their three-storey house looked out over the estuary where the River Aln flowed into the sea. It was, Iris was convinced at the time, the prettiest village in the world, with little stone houses, a glorious beach, golf courses, sand dunes, pubs and winding roads.

Her father bought a small boat and after that it was very difficult to get David out of it and her mother was perpetually standing down on the water's edge, worrying as fog came down in case they would be lost but she did not complain because they had to get Daddy away from work at weekends.

They had a steel foundry in Durham. As local businesses went it was quite a big affair and something went wrong almost every day and amazingly it was always something different, so her mother said.

David was the most important person in Iris's life. They made plans together of how when they got older they would have a house of their own and she would make wonderful cakes for him.

He had, she thought, the most wide beautiful eyes in the whole world. They were the same colour as her own, the kind of green which was nature's green like leaves on the trees, long grass in the orchard, the colour that says all the best things, emeralds, spring-time, new hope. God's own colour, her mother said. David had thick black lashes around his eyes.

Everybody liked him, he was so polite and quiet that sometimes she wished he would shout and throw his fists around like other boys did in the schoolyard but somehow David's quiet perseverance stilled people, stopped them.

If that didn't work he would leave the situation. It was not usually a retreat, it had too much dignity for that, rather as though he was bored with the situation and refused to continue or as if his time could be better spent on something more constructive.

When Iris was eleven she went to the girls' grammar school in the town. The most sig-nificant event of their childhood happened that year. David was seven. She came home one afternoon from spending the day at Wharton Park, which was situated in the north end of the town with a view of the cathedral and enough room to play for hours, with some friends, to find a huge trunk open in David's room and her mother seated by the window, sewing.

Iris gazed in at the door. It had been a long hot summer and she and David had enjoyed every day of it, weeks and weeks when they were free to picnic on the riverbanks, go boating and play games, lie under the trees in the garden and eat ice cream, drink lots of lemonade and on the odd rainy day they had retreated to the loft above the garage to read and tell stories.

'What are you doing?' she said.

Her mother looked up.

'I'm sewing name tapes into David's socks,' she said with a sigh, 'and tedious work it is too.'

'Why?'

'For when he goes to London to school in September, of course.'

Iris stared. She did remember that David had had several days off going looking at schools he should go to later but he had been vague when she asked and she had somehow assumed that whatever school he went to it was not terribly important. David was at the nearest primary school.

'He likes where he is.'

Her mother looked patiently at her.

'I know he does, dear, but boys of his age they go away.'

'Away where?'

'Don't be obtuse, Iris. Lots of your friends go to boarding school.'

'You're sending David to boarding school?'

Her mother stopped what she was doing and when she looked up her face was pale.

'Nothing of the kind,' she said, 'he agreed to it.'

'He's seven,' Iris pointed out.

'Now that you're here you can help with the name tapes.'

'David can't want to go.'

'He wouldn't want to be left out when all his friends do, would he?'

'Why aren't I there, then?'

'I thought you were happy to go to the grammar school.'

'I don't remember being given the option.'

'You didn't want to, as I recall,' her mother said.

She hadn't, her mother was right, she had been horrified at the idea of leaving Durham to go and live at school when it was bad enough having to go during the day. Why on earth people would want to stay there for whole weeks at a time she could not imagine, and unlike David she was vocal enough to make her views felt.

Iris ran down the stairs and into the garden where David was sitting with a couple of friends in the big fir tree at the bottom in the shade because it was such a hot day.

She couldn't talk to him in front of other small boys so she left it until later that evening and went into his bedroom when he came in from playing, he was dirty, tired, his lank hair hung over his eyes. His mother was running the bath.

'Are you really going to boarding school?' Iris said.

'It's not for ages yet.'

'Three weeks.'

'Is it?' He said nothing more.

'Do you want to go?'

David didn't reply. He didn't even look at her.

'They're sending you two hundred and fifty miles away. Was it one you liked?'

'I didn't like any of them,' David said.

'Did you say you liked it?'

'No, of course not.'

'Aren't you going to tell them you don't want to go?'

He shrugged and his skinny shoulders seemed to droop.

'Everybody goes,' he said, and then his mother called,

'David, your bath is ready. Hurry up before it gets cold.'

Iris wanted to ask him whether he had any idea what it would be like being so far from home for so long and on and off for years but she didn't because David obviously felt that he had no power here, there was nothing he could do or he did not want to disappoint his parents.

He went off to have his bath and she went downstairs to where her father was sitting in the garden in a big chair.

'You didn't tell me David was going to boarding school,' she said.

Her father gazed narrowly at her against

31

the sunlight.

'Nonsense, Iris, you knew about it months ago.'

'David doesn't want to go.'

Her father didn't answer.

'What am I supposed to do without him?' Iris said.

He didn't answer that either for a few moments and then he said,

'All his friends are going.'

'To the same school?'

Her father moved with impatience.

'No, not the same school but something like. He wouldn't want to be left out.'

After that the summer was spoiled. The pile of clothes on the floor in David's room got smaller as the trunk filled. Every morning Iris woke up and thought it was a day nearer to David's leaving and she dreaded it. She was at school on the morning that he left but she saw him before she went and he was all done up in his grey uniform with the purple and brown badge and his purple and brown tie. He looked so defenceless, so scared and Iris couldn't think of a single thing to say to him.

The house was like a different place without him and her life changed so much. She had lots of friends but there was nobody to confide in as she had with David and because it as such a long way he did not come home until Christmas.

She ran into the house from school on the day that he was coming back to discover another small boy playing trains with him.

'Hello, Iris.' David barely looked at her. 'This is Matthews. His parents are abroad so he's staying with us for Christmas.'

Matthews concentrated on getting the blue train back on to its tracks and didn't say anything.

That night Iris heard them talking and giggling in David's room. She had never felt so left out. She hadn't seen David since early September, he had not come home at half term, it was such a long way, her mother had explained, and he had gone to stay with their aunt and uncle who lived in London. Iris wanted to ask if her mother didn't miss him but somehow she didn't seem able. The following day she went into town with a friend from school, Janet Robson.

'But they're just little lads,' Janet said. 'Why would you want to spend your time with them?'

Things were never the same again. It was as though David disappeared into the crowd of small boys at his school and wasn't special any more. She was too old to be with boys of that age and from then on to Iris there was always somebody between them, her friends, his.

The secrets they had had, the games they had played and how they would lie in the big bed in her room at night and watch the car lights coming down the hill ... that was gone too. The precious years of childhood that she and David had had together were over.

David became taller, thinner, quieter. He never said anything about school, he never referred to it in the holidays and he had local friends that he went about with, lads he built bonfires with, had gangs, even fought from time to time in the streets of the city when he was thirteen and fourteen and there were always girls. Girls liked David.

Iris well remembered the day he was taller than her for the first time when he came home in the summer. After that he grew and she didn't so that she had to look up at him always and he was no longer her little brother. By the time David was seventeen he was over six feet tall and she was five foot three and there was nothing left of their relationship. She thought it would never recover.

Her friends liked him but David never liked them and he didn't like any of the boys she went out with so that they did not meet up socially and then suddenly it changed again, the summer that he was eighteen, when he left school and came home for the last time before university.

Two

Iris remembered clearly the time she had decided to become a nurse. It began on a warm summer's night and her parents were having a party. It was her mother's birthday. Her mother always had a party on her birthday. It was a nice tradition and her father was keen on the idea; this year was a particularly big event since her mother was fifty.

Her father had hired the County Hotel in Old Elvet, right in the middle of the city. It was the part of the town where the legal business went on, courts and solicitors' offices and further over the prison, but it had wonderful buildings, including half a dozen small pubs and several hotels, the County being one of the best with its back looking out over the widest street there and its other side facing the River Wear.

Her mother had fussed about what they should wear. Iris didn't care about such things and was impatient, especially when she saw her reflection in the mirror of her bedroom. The dress was pink silk and had tiny velvet bows. It was, she thought, hideous, like she was a little girl on an outing. Her mother looked much better, she wore silk chiffon in summer colours, red and yellow, delicate.

There was a band, people were dancing and the windows were open to the warm evening sky. All their friends had come and a lot of young people whom her parents considered her friends but they weren't really, Iris thought. The trouble was that she didn't like her parents' friends' children.

All the young men seemed to think about was sport and whether they could get their hands on you and all the young women talked about was marriage and domestic issues and clothes and Iris acknowledged to herself that she had not one single good friend, nobody to confide in, nobody she really liked.

She went outside. Janet followed her, they were still friends, though Iris was rather tired of Janet, she was just like the others. Janet clutched her arm.

'Did you see him?'

'Who?'

Janet looked at her in despair.

'Don't you ever notice anybody? Johnny Fenwick is here.' Iris looked blankly at her. 'They're seriously rich. I didn't know you knew the Fenwicks.'

'We don't. My father does business with his father, that's all.'

'He came alone,' Janet said and she didn't mean without his parents, she meant without a girl.

Iris shrugged her off. Janet went back inside. She walked away down the path. A young man was standing watching the river. His fair hair blew about in the slight breeze. He was smoking a cigarette and turned, as though startled, when she joined him.

'Don't worry,' she said, 'I haven't come to disturb you. I'm trying to get out of the way.'

'Me too,' he said. 'Ghastly party, isn't it?'

'Awful,' Iris agreed.

'Do you know these people?'

'Who?'

'The Blacks. They have a daughter they are keen to marry off. I don't want to get entangled with anybody.'

'Oh, there isn't much chance of that,' Iris said, 'she wouldn't marry you if you were the last man on earth.'

He stared for a few seconds, about to be embarrassed, and then choked, threw down his cigarette, put his foot on it and started to laugh. It was a pleasant infectious sound but Iris failed to be impressed.

'I'm most awfully sorry,' he said.

'Oh, go and bugger yourself,' Iris said and she went back inside.

She cried, that was the worst part, that people thought she was up for grabs, like a slab of butter on a shelf, and it wasn't true, at least not to her. She wanted badly to go home and worst of all, when she came out of the ladies' room there he was, looking penitent.

'Forgive me. Dance with me.'

'Why?'

'I'm so frightfully sorry, it's just that people know who I am and it doesn't help.'

'I don't know who you are. You haven't ever been to the parties I've been to before.'

'I've just finished at university. I'm Johnny Fenwick.'

'Oh hell, are you?' Iris said.

'I wasn't going to come back here but I was worried about my father.'

'Why?'

'My mother died and ... all he ever does is work now.'

'I'm sorry,' Iris said.

'Would you like to dance?'

So they did and the trouble was, Iris thought afterwards, that was the moment I fell in love with him. So much for plans and decisions.

He danced well enough so that she wanted to dance with him again. It had become the night of her life. Iris had always scorned girls who fell in love, she thought them weak and stupid, how they had known the exact moment and what it was like afterwards.

She danced with him the entire evening and when it was time to say goodnight she wished and wished that he would kiss her and when he did not she wished that he would ask to see her again and when he did not do that either she had to stop herself from asking him whether she could see him.

Alone in her room when the last of other partygoers, who had come back to the house afterwards, were calling goodnight in the street well beyond the house, Iris was angry with herself.

There was a discreet knocking on the door and when she murmured something her mother put her head round the door and then came into the room, closing the door behind her as though she had something important to say.

'Iris...' she said and hesitated.

'I know. I know. I shouldn't have danced every dance with him. It looked so obvious.'

Her mother seemed surprised.

'Shouldn't you have? I rather liked the look of him. Are you seeing him again?'

Iris could have laughed at herself for her prissy notions. All her mother wanted was a good gossip.

'I don't know. He didn't say.'

Her mother hesitated for a few moments and then she said, 'Be careful, won't you?'

'What do you mean?'

'Rich people are different.'

'There is nothing to worry about. I have no intention of marrying him. Mother, what would you say if I said I thought I might like to be a nurse?'

Her mother looked even more surprised.

'Do you?' she said.

'I'd like to do something.'

Her mother sat down on the bed as though two surprises was rather too much.

'Well, I don't suppose anybody could have any objection.'

'I thought you wanted me to marry.'

'I do but perhaps not quite yet. You are still young. It's how I want you to end up but not necessarily how I want you to start out. Nursing is a very hard thing to do. If you want to do something why not become a teacher? You could go to college and...' She stopped there because Iris was shaking her head.

'I couldn't possibly teach but I might see myself as a nurse.'

'I suppose we could think about it,' her mother said, looking rather disappointed.

'What will Daddy say?'

'He only wants you to be happy.'

It was three days later when Iris had gone into town shopping and she came home to find Johnny Fenwick seated on her mother's sofa, drinking tea and making small talk. She saw the relief in her mother's eyes as she came in. Her mother got up.

'There you are,' she said, 'perhaps you would like to give Mr Fenwick some more tea. I must go and see to the dinner,' and she excused herself and went off.

Iris picked up the teapot and as she did he said hastily, 'I've had three cups already, thank you.'

'Battenberg?'

'I've had two pieces.'

Iris poured tea for herself and said to him, 'To what do we owe this pleasure?'

He grinned in embarrassment.

'I wondered if you might like to go out with me. Maybe you'd like to go for a walk or a drink or to a dance?'

'I might,' Iris said. 'When did you have in mind?'

'How about now?'

And she had been unable to say no somehow. Her friends would have cast up their eyes at her naivety. You never said yes straight away like that, it gave young men the wrong impression.

They walked on the towpath by the riverbanks first, it was a lovely day, and later, when it rained, they went to the cinema and then they went to the Queen Victoria pub in Hallgarth Street which was a winding road leading south out of the city. The pub had not been changed from when it was originally built and had a tiny bar and she took him to the Dun Cow further along Elvet, one of the oldest parts of the city, a three-hundred-year-old pub where the young

41

people often congregated. It had low ceilings and very good beer.

Later still they went dancing at the County where they had met and Iris had not forgotten the bliss of being so close and she had the joy of being even closer since her parents were not there, she was not at home and the music was slow and soft. They sat outside later, watching the river go past and the people cross Elvet Bridge.

At the end of the evening, in the darkness, not far from her house, Johnny finally took her into his arms and kissed her. Iris had been kissed before but it had not felt like this, it had not mattered. When the kiss was over he followed it by another and then another and then he said,

'May I see you tomorrow?'

She tried to think.

'Please,' he prompted her.

'Then yes.'

She floated inside. Her parents were still up and she felt obliged to call into the sitting room to tell them she was home and all her mother said was,

'Did you have a nice evening, dear?' and Iris said that she had and wished them goodnight.

She didn't sleep. Part of her wanted to go back to never having met him because she already sensed how complicated it had become but mostly she just wanted to lie there and think of how he made her feel, of the sweetness of his mouth and the smoothness of his body under her hands.

They saw each other every day that week, they played tennis, they went walking, they sat outside pubs drinking gin and tonic and on the Saturday he said to her, 'Would you like to go back to my house? The housekeeper has gone away for a few days and there's nobody in.'

'Won't your father be there?'

'He had to go away on business. We could have a drink and...'

Curious to see how he lived, Iris agreed. They drove to a tiny village only a few miles away to the north of the city, through huge gates and there was a castle. It was enormous, grey stone, and was deserted. It was falling down, in such bad repair that it seemed strange anyone should want to live there.

There were odd walls and towers spread over a vast area and she remembered seeing it from the road, she had always thought it looked rather like sea horses, its towers half built from the twelfth century or something like that, she couldn't remember. She shivered, in spite of the summer day. It made her think of ghosts and times past.

He stopped the car, led her up stone steps and inside through double doors. The rooms were enormous, high and wide with great big floor-to-ceiling windows and great long corridors.

He did not hesitate. He took her into his arms the very second the door was closed and Iris had known that he was going to and could not have waited any longer for him to do so. And when the kiss was done, he said, very close to her mouth,

'I want you, Iris. Will you go to bed with me?'

And she said,

'Yes.'

How simple. How strange. She had been holding off men and boys since she was fourteen, never being alone with them, never letting them do any more than kiss her, but she felt as though she could not refuse Johnny Fenwick anything.

She had waited for him to try to put his hands on her, to see how far he could get before she refused and stopped him but he had not done that and his honesty disarmed Iris. There was something about the straight-forwardness of it which made her unable even to think of refusing.

They went up two flights of stairs arm in arm and into a very big bedroom and there the curtains were open to the night and there was a view of the river and the cath-edral, outlined against the sky, black in the very far distance and nearer there were fields.

Iris did not care about the view or the town or the fact that she was doing something which potentially might ruin her, both by reputation and if she should become pregnant when she was not married.

She didn't care about anything. She loved the recklessness of it and she loved him. The whole idea of having somebody for hers was so delicious, so wonderful that she abandoned her principles as she never had before.

He told her he loved her though he needn't have done, she didn't care. She was only happy when they were both naked, when they had pulled one another's clothes off and there in the big firm bed with the starlight, the moonlight flooding the room with a pure white sheen, she finally got him as close as he could be, as close as she wanted. In the silence of the big house all around, Iris was ecstatic. He only paused to say,

'I'm not hurting you, am I?' and his voice was almost confident so that Iris laughed and said,

'You couldn't hurt me.' She was to remember it but in circumstances like these it was true. She knew with confidence that he would never hurt her in this way, that they were meant to be together, that it would always be wonderful. The night was hers.

Much later he put on a lamp by the bed and went downstairs and brought up cold champagne, sweet and bitter bubbles, and wide-mouthed long-stemmed glasses. They drank the champagne in bed and Iris thought if she never saw another night, if she never had such a time again, it didn't matter now. She had had everything.

'I love you so very much, Johnny Fenwick,' she said, how good to be able to say it and care nothing for the consequences.

'Do you really?'

'You sound as though you believe me.'

'I do. And I love you. I shall never ever love anyone again like I love you now. I knew the minute I saw you and you swore at me.'

Iris laughed.

They made love again and they slept. In the morning they sat outside in the garden and ate scrambled eggs in the sunlight.

'I suppose you should have gone home,' he said.

'I suppose I should have,' she said, not caring.

She got up and did a little dance on the lawn and he kissed her and then they went back to bed. Later she telephoned her mother and lied for the first time, saying she had stayed at a friend's and her mother said that she was not to worry and she laughed and said they had not noticed she had not come home, had gone to bed early and how negligent did that make them as parents?

It was a sign, she said, of all their maturity, and just to come back when she was ready.

Would it be today? It would not. Iris said she had no idea when it might be and she hoped that her parents didn't mind. Her mother assured her that they did not. Iris, however, had the feeling that her mother knew exactly what was going on but chose not to say anything which she could only be relieved about and rather astonished.

Three

Jack Fenwick walked into the castle and for once in his life was glad to be there in the place which had been his father's delight. He had affection for the building. Parts of it had been falling down for centuries and were still doing so, spread over an acre or so of the hundred acres which comprised the land he still owned there. There were grey stones everywhere, steps which led nowhere, ruins which had been rooms open now to the sky, the odd fireplace perched precariously against half-built walls.

The main part of it which still stood consisted of two dozen rooms or so, mended and re-mended over five centuries with dungeons and cellars and a vast hall where once the local aristocrats had ridden their horses into before it was roofed and two fireplaces were installed.

From it two winding stone staircases rose into the first floor where more practical places like the big kitchen, the dining room, the library, the study and the drawing room were situated. The bedrooms were up another flight of stairs, half a dozen of them with views right across the countryside, of the Wear silver beyond as it wended its way toward the city and the fields where creamy sheep nibbled the grass, horses stood under the trees with caramel-coloured cattle and around it all the crisscross fencing which people recognized as the limits of his domain.

The morning was hot. In here it was cool and the outside door echoed as he slammed it. Peace, silence, retreat. It was eight o'clock. He had driven through the night to get home. He could have been driven, he could have taken a train but he just wanted to be by himself, to think, to sit with the hood down on the Daimler and drive into the morning and not think about anything.

He wanted tea and toast. There was nobody here but he was not too tired to do such things, though he would have given a great deal to be in his bed. He walked up the stairs and along the wide hall towards the kitchen. The dining-room door stood open. That room had been his wife's favourite place.

He paused there and then could hardly breathe. Standing by the big doors which led out on to the balcony in the sunshine was a woman and for several seconds he thought it was Anna, the way she stood, the long bare legs. His whole body felt like it was lit and then common sense squashed the illusion. She was very young, as Anna had looked when they first met, unused, fresh and then she heard or sensed him and turned around and she was not Anna, she had dark hair instead of fair, green eyes instead of blue and was nowhere near as tall.

She looked confused, embarrassed and she was beautiful, with pale skin and full lips. She wore a white shirt, no doubt something she had put on as nothing more than a covering so most likely she was somebody Johnny had brought home, they had probably just got out of bed. He felt envy, lust, self-pity and then had enough sense to go forward, hand outstretched and say, casually,

'How do you do? I'm Johnny's father, Jack Fenwick.'

'Oh,' she said and then regained her composure and he admired how swiftly she did so.

'Would you like tea and toast?' he offered.

'I would love some,' she said.

Iris retreated swiftly up the stairs. She was ready to panic. Whatever would Johnny's father think? He hadn't looked upset but any parent would be, to find a strange girl in the house at this hour and wearing nothing but one of his son's shirts so that it was obvious that she had spent the night and what they had been doing. Her face went warm.

She thought back to the man in the doorway as she had turned around. She could picture him, tall and lean and wearing a suit but not a tie, a crumpled suit, as though he had travelled a long way.

He looked tired, his eyes narrowed beneath straight dark hair and she liked that he looked at her face and not at her legs as most men would have done and yet it had been a frankly admiring look.

She gazed at Johnny sleeping. He looked very young, not as though he was her lover, as though he was just a boy, and she wished just a little, for the first time, that she had not stayed a second night. It mattered now and the idyll was over. Was that because his father had come home and the reality took the magic away? Johnny looked nothing like his father, that was the second shock of the morning, he must take after his mother, fair and blue-eyed.

As she reached the bed Johnny opened his eyes.

'Your father's home,' she said.

Johnny closed his eyes again. Iris shook him.

'Whatever will he think?'

Johnny opened his eyes again but reluctantly.

'He has too much to think about to care about what we're doing,' he said. 'Besides, if he's here now it's because he's driven all night from London. He does it a lot and he's always worn out when he gets here. Don't worry about the old man, he won't care and besides, it's none of his business what we do.'

Iris considered staying upstairs. What a very awkward situation except that the tall dark man in the doorway hadn't seemed very surprised to see her.

'Do you often bring girls back here?' she said to Johnny now.

'No, of course not,' he said impatiently and turned over away from her.

Iris put on her underwear and her pale cream linen dress and followed the smell of hot toast to the kitchen and from there into the dining room. The French windows were open to the summer morning and sunshine was pouring across the balcony.

In the garden below the windows were blue cornflowers and orange poppies, tall and quite still because there was no breeze, growing there in among the ruins as though they had a duty to do so. The grass had been left deliberately long there, she thought, and the view went down past the gardens towards the river. Lots of trees were in full green foliage.

He had put china and cutlery on to the table out there and was even now coming out of the kitchen with a teapot and a toast rack on a tray. There was also a butter dish, a big piece of honeycomb and a bowl of oranges.

'Sit down,' he offered and as he distributed the various things from the tray on to the table Iris looked at him.

He was not as old as her father nor like the

other fathers she had seen and he didn't act anything like fathers did or like the very powerful person he was supposed to be, he behaved like somebody who was used to looking after himself though she was sure that wasn't true.

She tried to think what he did, or how he was very rich, but she either didn't know or couldn't remember. The rich men she had seen so far in her life were stuffy older people with moustaches who had servants and spoke like the royal family and were from a different world. He was not like that. He was an industrialist, she remembered, a man who worked. That made her feel better somehow.

He poured out tea and pushed the milk jug at her, told her to help herself. The toast was thick, warm and brown, butter dripping on to the plate and the honey on to her fingers. She ate two huge pieces before she considered anything more.

'You didn't tell me your name,' he said and she thought he had beautiful eyes, keen and intelligent.

'Iris Black.'

'Oh, are you?' He studied her and she thought she would never have known him for Johnny's father, pale skin where Johnny's face was tanned, eyes almost black and thick straight black hair. Were all middle-aged men this self-assured? Her father's friends weren't like this. They called her stupid things like 'young lady' and made ridiculous jokes as though they didn't know what to say and they leered at her. 'Ah, yes, I know. You're the steel-founder's daughter. You look like your father.'

'Have you met him?'

'We do business together, at least our companies do. He's a good man.'

Iris thought it was a particularly kind thing to say, even though her father was well known for his generosity.

'Thank you.'

The dew on the lawns was beginning to dry as the sun took over the day.

'What a beautiful place,' Iris said.

'The view's nice,' he said, 'the place is going to rack and ruin.'

The way that he said it made Iris laugh.

'It's meant to be like that, it would spoil it if you propped it up, it's beautiful in its own special way and it's your house,' she said.

'It was my father's idea. I don't know why I keep it. Sentiment maybe. I'm never here.'

'But you have ... your business is here.'

'Part of it is in Newcastle. The headquarters is in London. I come here occasionally for some peace since...'

He didn't say 'since my wife died' and Iris knew nothing of death so she didn't say anything. He got up, said,

'Please excuse me. I haven't slept. Do help yourself to anything you would like. Don't run away because I'm here. I shall get up at teatime and go to Newcastle for a few days and you will have the house to yourselves. I hope I'll see you again,' and he was gone.

Jack went up the big wide stairs, his footsteps echoing. If ever he had the time to attend to it, he thought, he must sell this monument to his father's achievements. He could not stop himself from thinking about Anna and the pretty terraced house in Edinburgh where they had gone for peace. He had not sold that either, always he made excuses. He did not even have to become involved. All he had to do was to say to Mrs Gibson, his secretary, 'I want to sell the Edinburgh house and the castle. Sort it out, would you?'

It was one of the benefits of wealth like his. You didn't have to do any of the detail, you could pay somebody else to do it. And yet he did not. He dismissed it from his mind as he reached his bedroom. He was so very tired. He was beginning to think he would never eat or sleep again without thinking of work but at least it stopped him from thinking about Anna and how much he missed her and how badly he wanted her.

He had not been thinking about her when he came home. And then he had seen Iris Black standing in the morning sunlight. She was not a tall girl yet her bare legs seemed so long and he was aware of her body beneath the shirt.

When she turned around her green eyes were as hard and brilliant as emeralds and her hair was shiny clean and made him remember what being young was like, energy and ambition and confidence because you knew so little.

Jack despised men of his age who wanted young women. He told himself heatedly now that it was typical. You should never despise other people because you were only ever one step away from such things yourself.

How sad, how disgusting to feel like that about the girl his son was obviously sleeping with but he had liked the challenge in her eyes and there was something about the way she turned and her mouth that reminded him of Anna.

He called himself names now as he pulled off his clothes. It was just that he was exhausted and that Johnny had brought a lovely girl to the house and the place was the better for women.

All houses should have women in them and this place had been without a woman for years. Before he passed into blissful unconsciousness he thought that Johnny had never brought a girl home before. If she was to be important then he must get used to her and he was glad that Johnny had found such a woman. He was just sorry for himself and for all the other men who didn't have a woman like Iris Black.

Those long bare legs invaded his dreams and made his body ache for Anna and when he awoke he remembered the months when Anna had fought the cancer which consumed her body.

After she died there had been a discreet silence of about three months and after that a deluge of invitations in London, in Newcastle and even here in Durham. Other people could not wait to marry him off to some poor unsuspecting bitch who imagined he had affection to give anybody.

Everywhere he went men and mothers threw their sisters and daughters at him because of who he was and all that money and there had been times when he had almost given in and married some woman who was witty or had kind eyes or a decent pair of breasts for him to hide in but always he saw Anna's face, her mocking glance. He had never again felt that wonderful freedom from his own bloody intellect that told him he was not alone, that he had managed to recapture the kind of love which was once so abundantly his. Until today, when Iris Black stood all unsuspecting by the window.

How strange. He knew nothing about her. It was not even, in spite of his body's response, an entirely physical thing, it was just the release of tedium, the knowing that however many hours, days, weeks, months and years he should spend with her he would never be bored, his life would take on that champagne quality of being carried a little way above the earth, in the arms of requited love.

He turned over in bed and laughed bitterly at himself. You stupid old bugger, he said, you can still be taken in by the cruelty of life and played like a bloody salmon.

Iris stayed there for four days. Then Johnny took her home. They left the car at a long distance and he walked her over Framwellgate Bridge under the eyes of the castle and the cathedral, up the narrow twisting cobbled road, past the shops and the café. There they kissed under the brightness of the stars.

Arm in arm, they walked up Silver Street and into the market place and up the hill to where her house lay above the little city and the river.

He left her at the door. It was late and Iris regretted his leaving. When he had gone, when she had seen him out of sight, she went inside. Her parents had gone to bed. The house was in darkness save for the light in the hall which they had left burning for her.

She liked that they had left it burning, she liked in a way that she could accept and love his leaving of her, that she would see him again. She went to bed and lay there, thinking what fun they had had at the castle.

She went to sleep smiling, hugging the pillow to her because she was no longer used to sleeping alone. How quickly she had grown used to the curve of his body, the neatness of his breathing, the smoothness of his shoulders beneath her mouth. She slept sweetly in the knowledge that she would see him again the following day.

Johnny and his father had always been close. He was his only child. His mother had been ill on and off for years. She had suffered from cancer for more than two years before she died. He had been at university then and had, he was ashamed to think of it now, stayed away from his homes both here and in London and Edinburgh as much as possible, he had hated that she was ill, that he might lose her.

Now he wanted somebody to talk to and it seemed to him that since his father was at home he might ask him something important.

He knocked, and hearing his father's voice, walked into the study where his father very often worked. It was a good room, walled with leather-bound volumes, easy chairs grouped around the fire and then around a desk and some of those wonderful revolving bookshelves here and there and low lights and a view of the garden down the lawns and beyond the trees, and in the distance the tall tower of the cathedral grey.

'Can I talk to you?' he said.

His father put down his pen.

'Have a seat,' he invited and Johnny sat down in the comfortable chair with big arms at this side of the desk. 'Want some whisky?'

Johnny nodded. His father was obviously glad of the interruption. He got up and went over to the cabinet on the back wall where a decanter and glasses stood on a tray and he poured whisky into big heavy glasses and passed one across the desk and then he sat down again. It was a single malt, smooth. Johnny took two big gulps and swallowed hard before he said,

'I want to get married.'

His father looked at him and Johnny waited for him to say 'You're too young' or 'It's very sudden' or 'Are you sure you've thought about it' but he didn't. He sat for a few moments and then he said,

'Iris Black?'

'Yes. You don't seem surprised.'

His father frowned and then relaxed.

'We had breakfast together. Nice family. Have you asked her?'

'Not yet. I wanted to know what you think.'

'Well, if you like her that's good enough for me. I'll buy you a house.'

'Wonderful.'

'Can't have you living in this dump.' It wasn't quite the way most people would have referred to the castle. 'Go ahead and ask her.'

'Thanks, Dad, I'll go over tomorrow.'

Jack waited until his son left the room and then he finished the whisky and poured another before reminding himself that he had a great deal of work to do and had to be able to think. He sat there, not drinking the second measure, swearing at himself and thinking what a bloody fool he was. He didn't understand why Iris Black had made such an impression on him and it was not the impression he wanted anybody, any woman to make. She reminded him how alone he was, how lonely – that was the first time he had admitted it.

He knew enough to be aware that women preferred rich men. Why not? They would be stupid not to. Money made life so much easier and women had few choices. Some women pretended they weren't interested, some weren't interested and he never regretted them, some felt like he did, some just wanted to be looked after, some saw themselves as providers of homes while men went out and did the dull bits. Some saw him as a potential father even at forty, he thought with a wince. It was not old, it just felt old.

He had loved only once, he was beginning to think that love was rationed, had grown used to the idea that although he could lust after any beautiful body he would never marry again, he might never even become involved with anyone, that he wanted to take no one home with him. Why then was it that he should be so interested in the woman his son wanted to marry? It was disgusting at best. At its worst it was ... he didn't want to think about it.

He had wanted to say to Johnny that he was far too young to consider marriage but since he had been married himself when he was eighteen – much against his parents' wishes – he could hardly tell his son not to. And it had been the right thing to do. The difference was that his father was not tortured with stupid visions of the woman his son wanted to marry, at least as far as I know, he thought with a laugh. Maybe I'm wrong, maybe most men lust after the young women their sons fall in love with.

In earlier times he might have drunk the whisky down in one and thrown the glass at the fireplace but he knew it for a stupid thing. His secretary, Tamsin Gibson, who had followed him north, had stayed on that evening to work so she would be aware of it, she was only in the next room. So he didn't, he just sat there and called himself names until she came in some minutes later.

'You should have gone home an hour ago,' he said.

She looked reprovingly at him. 'I should have done nothing of the sort,' she said.

'You have a whole pile of invitations–'

'Say no to all of them.'

Mrs Gibson ignored him.

'Sir Alfred and Lady Willoughby's–'

'No.'

'The Lord Mayor's–'

'No.'

'Mr–'

'No.'

She stopped and looked at him again over the top of her spectacles.

'You don't even know what I was about to say.'

'It doesn't matter.'

'You never go anywhere,' she said.

'You never go anywhere either. Do I tell you that you should?'

'You are not my secretary.'

'That, Mrs Gibson, is one of the few things I am extremely thankful for. We are in the north-east for a week. Why don't you go home to your husband while you have the opportunity?'

She hesitated and then she said,

'Do you really think there will be a war?'

He closed his eyes for a second.

'Not for a very long time, if ever. Stop worrying. I think we are producing armaments for no reason, working without incentive. You and I may be out of a job soon.'

'You are not funny,' she said. 'And you drink too much.'

'Please. Go home.'

Mrs Gibson hesitated. Her husband was thirty. Jack knew that if it came to war at some time in the future her husband and his son would both be fighting probably with the very weapons he was making. There was something awful in it. There was something worse in the idea that there would not be the right weapons for the job, aircraft too big for accuracy, tanks which became immobilized by water, guns which jammed. These things were his nightmare.

'You will try to get some sleep?' she said.

Jack smiled at her. After Johnny she was the most important person in his life. She was twenty-eight. She was beautiful, glamorous, blonde, had gorgeous legs and a mind like a needle. He didn't fancy her one little bit. He had that at least to be thankful for. She earned a huge salary and was worth it. He could not manage without her.

'And no more whisky tonight,' she said as she went out.

He waited until she was gone and then finished the golden liquid in his glass over the next hour or so and got up and poured himself another generous measure. He couldn't manage without it any longer, not if he was to work most of the night which he almost always did.

Johnny wanted to get this right, it was his

first proposal and he was hoping it would be his last. He went to the foundry, the works, he wasn't quite sure what it was but he didn't want to wait until Mr Black was at home because he wanted to be sure of seeing him alone so he drove to the big iron gates, left his car outside and trod up the dusty path to the offices. It wasn't a big place, which surprised him rather, but then the Blacks weren't rich, they were respectable business people.

A young woman was sitting at a desk just inside the door as though to politely ward people off. Johnny stopped there.

'I'm Johnny Fenwick,' he said. 'I wondered whether I might have a quick word with Mr Black.'

'He's in his office. If you wait a moment I'll go and ask.'

She disappeared into the shadows at the back and almost immediately returned and ushered him through. Iris's father remembered him from the party. Johnny was surprised.

He shook his hand and said he was glad to see him and Johnny thought that even though the desk was covered in papers Mr Black was pleased to see him and he was glad to think he might be part of such a family. He had not had that.

He thought back to the party, Mrs Black smiling and greeting people and how affable they seemed and it made him think of his mother's death and how lonely he and his father had been since then. There was a part of him which ached for a family to belong to.

Mr Black had kind eyes but shrewd too. He waited without saying anything and Johnny wished it were easier to talk about such things as this. He could not think whether Mr Black would be pleased that he wanted to marry Iris or not. Did they know anything about him? He suspected they didn't.

'I'm sorry to interrupt you,' Johnny said.

'Not at all. Do sit down. What can I do for you?'

'It's a little bit awkward,' Johnny said.

'Tea always helps,' Mr Black said.

'Yes, but you might not like what I'm going to say.'

'Oh dear. Then you'd better say it quickly.'

'I want to marry Iris,' Johnny said.

Mr Black looked astonished.

'I do think we should have some tea,' he said and he went into the outer office and spoke to the young woman and then he came back.

Johnny had been all wrong about them. He had thought they wanted to marry Iris off. Now Mr Black looked as though he didn't or as though he might be worried that Johnny wasn't good enough for her.

'Would you have any objections?' he said.

'You do know who I am? I mean, that sounds

silly but perhaps you don't and you think I'm
... some philanderer, adventurer, something
ridiculous like that but I ... I'm not...' Johnny
stopped there, he felt sweaty and was bab-
bling, he was so nervous. All he could do was
to look appealingly at Iris's father and mut-
ter,

'Would you mind?'

'Not at all if it's what you both want.'

Oh, how polite. Johnny was weak with
relief.

'I haven't asked her yet,' he admitted. 'I do
care for her very much and I think I will be
able to afford a wife. My father has offered
to buy us a house.'

'That's very generous. Have you known
one another long?'

'Do you think it matters?'

'I shouldn't think so. I knew the minute I
saw her mother that I wanted to marry her.
Still would have made the same decision but
you have to be sure.'

'I am sure,' Johnny said, confident of
something for the first time in his life. 'I love
Iris and I think I could make her happy. I
feel that I shall never love anyone again as I
love her and I would very much like her to
be my wife but I wanted to be sure that you
didn't mind.'

'I don't mind as long as you will look after
Iris.'

'What about Mrs Black?'

'I don't think she will mind either as long as it's what Iris wants,' he said and then the tea came and they drank it with relief.

Iris slept late. Her mother came in to wake her and pulled back the curtains and let in the sunlight and Iris turned over in half consciousness as her mother paused. She sat down on the bed.

'Are you awake?'

'Mm.'

'Iris, what are you doing?'

She lay for a few seconds, considered the question and then sat up, carefully because she was naked, not the way she usually slept.

'What do you mean?'

Her mother, looking far too wide awake, said,

'I haven't told your father but I know what's going on. You do know, don't you, that if you go to bed with a man before you're married that he will never ask you to marry him.'

She laughed and then saw her mother's face darken and she said, 'Oh, I'm sorry. It's just that I love him so very much and I wanted him.'

She watched the colour rush to her mother's cheeks because no respectable woman would say such a thing but she answered equably,

'That's all very well but...'

'Don't worry. It will be all right.'

'Do you know, I always worry twice as much when people say that,' her mother said, getting up. 'Johnny Fenwick is not ... there's nothing average about the Fenwicks and I have the impression they live differently. I would hate you to make some awful mistake, to fall in love while this ... boy is just playing games.'

Iris wanted to laugh again but her mother would have been offended so she just shook her head.

'Do come downstairs,' her mother said. 'It's almost midday and your father will be back for his dinner soon. I would hate to have to lie to him as to your whereabouts.'

It was strange to get up and have dinner. What she wanted was bacon and eggs, toast and coffee, honey, marmalade or warm strawberry jam, to taste her lover's mouth with butter on it, slick, sweet. The idea of toast and honey reminded her of Johnny's father somehow and that was not a comfortable thought. Men that age had no right to be interesting and attractive. She dismissed him from her mind.

Her father talked of work. She and her mother ploughed their way through what Iris barely recognized as wonderful little pies, full of beef with gravy and carrots and potatoes. She was so glad when her father went back to work and she could go back to thinking about Johnny.

She wanted to reassure her mother since a frosty air had settled between them but as the day wore on she didn't feel as though she had anything more to say which would help.

That evening she thought she heard some kind of commotion when she was upstairs, wondering if he would come and what they would do and regretting that his father was home and they could not spend the night in the castle which was so cool, quiet and empty.

Her mother came upstairs, all smiles.

'Mr Fenwick is here.'

Iris jumped up from the dressing table where she had been sitting, wondering possibly for the first time ever whether her simple print black-and-white summer dress looked good on her, and went downstairs into the hall and Johnny was there, smiling and he guided her into the billiard room and there he said to her,

'I've asked your father for your hand. I know it might seem very old-fashioned but I wanted to do the right thing.'

Iris stared at him. She went on staring at him, ignoring what he was saying to her. What had he been thinking of? The love between them was private, it was a secret, not something to be taken out and aired like damp washing. She did not want her parents to know, she did not want anybody involved in what went on between the two of them, it was hers, the only thing she had which belonged to her.

'I love you, Iris. Will you marry me?'

No wonder her mother had been so pleased, to know that things would soon so surely be resolved.

'Marry you?' She stared at him. 'But I thought you didn't want to get married.'

'That was before I got to know you. Please marry me, Iris. I love you so very much.'

She didn't know what to say, she wanted to say stupid things like how sudden it was and how she would have to think about it but she didn't.

'I don't want to get married,' she said in the sudden realization that it was true. How odd. She really didn't.

Johnny stared back at her.

'I thought you... I thought you cared about me.'

'I do. I want us to have some fun. I don't want all that responsibility, houses and – and babies and ... and besides, I want to train to be a nurse.' She didn't realize until that moment that she had already made up her mind.

Johnny stood, looking younger and younger by the second and more and more frustrated.

'This is ridiculous,' he said, 'every woman

wants to get married. Not being married and ... and having the kind of thing we have ... surely that's not what you want. If I've been instrumental in that I didn't mean to be. I wasn't trying to get away with anything, Iris, I ... I want you to marry me so that we can wake up together every day and we can have fun.'

'Fun? I don't think marriage and houses and babies is much fun. It certainly doesn't look it. That's what my parents are doing. I don't want that.'

He stood in the middle of the floor for some time, looking confused and then he left. Iris didn't move. Suddenly there was no one to turn to. She wished she and David were still close. Her mother came softly into the room.

'What happened?' she said.

Iris burst into tears.

'He spoiled it.' She wanted the secret, she wanted a love affair. Did that make her stupid or immoral? She wanted to sneak behind people's backs if necessary, she didn't want her parents being pleased and his father perhaps arranging to have the wedding at their dreadful castle and arrangements and dresses and everybody involved and flowers and bridesmaids and gossip.

She would have to have her own house and organize it and think about curtains and what they were to eat that week and go to the butcher's and learn to cook and even, oh horrors, become pregnant and get fat and feel sick and give birth. And then never ever have any time to herself again and not get to do the things she felt she so badly wanted to do.

She was an awful person, she knew it now. She did not want what other people wanted, she wanted fun and illicit arrangements and to have Johnny Fenwick all to herself and now she never would have. She ran away from her mother, she stayed in her room in the evening and when her parents wanted to talk to her she said that she would rather not just at the moment and they left her alone.

The following day she was lying in the shade of a big tree in the garden in a deck-chair when she heard somebody coming across the grass to her. It was David. He had been staying with friends in London. He hardly ever came home now and would be going to Edinburgh University in the autumn. We scarcely know one another any more, he never gives me any of his time, Iris thought.

'Hello, David, bored in London, were you?'

'I hear you turned down Johnny Fenwick,' he said.

Iris took off her sunglasses. David always came straight to the point. She was not sure she wanted to talk about it any more. She had cried until her eyes were swollen and David had not been there when she had needed him. He was never there when she needed him, she thought bitterly. But she knew that it was her own fault, nobody else's.

'I love him,' she said, 'but I don't want to start and play at houses.'

There was a second and then David said exactly the right thing, just as he had always done.

'Yes, quite,' he said, 'there are lots of other things to do before that,' and she was so relieved, so pleased, so glad that he was there.

'You think I was right, then.'

'I think you're only ready to get married when you are and as you are so obviously not, it would be the worst thing ever.'

'What do Mother and Daddy say?'

'I think she's disappointed but you'd already told her that you were making other plans, that you were thinking about becoming a nurse. They think it would have been much worse if you'd married him and then changed your mind. Don't worry about it, your instincts got you to the right place. Be glad.'

It was only later when they were sitting outside together such as they had not done for years and the sun was sinking beyond the garden that David said to her, 'You do know he'll marry somebody else and soon.'

'Do you think so?'

'Once people have such things in mind, when it's the right time of their lives, they look for somebody. The trouble is you and Johnny are out of time.'

She remembered it later, out of time was what they were and there was nothing anybody could do about it.

Four

Johnny stormed back into the castle and clashed the heavy oak door as hard as he could and went through into the enormous room where his father sat by the window, doing some kind of paperwork.

'She wouldn't have me,' Johnny said and his voice echoed into the vast ceiling.

His father stopped writing, looked up.

His father didn't say the things that Johnny was beginning to say to himself, that it was perhaps too soon, that he and Iris could have got to know one another much better before he asked but surely it wouldn't have made any difference. Didn't you know when you wanted to marry somebody? He had.

'Couldn't you wait? She will probably change her mind in time.'

I don't want to wait. He didn't say it out loud, it would have sounded childish but it was the truth. Since his mother had died and his father had gone away more often he was lonely as he had never been.

'I wanted us to be together, to do things together, to...'

'I felt like that about your mother.'

'I don't understand why she didn't want

what I want. That sounds stupid, I know, but women aren't like men. I mean they are supposed to be the ones who want to get married. She cares about me, I know she does so having...' He stumbled a bit here and had to take a couple of deep breaths before he could go on, he was just beginning to realize what had happened. 'Having thought she wanted to get married... I did what seemed the right thing and went to her father and he was pleased and her mother too, but ... it didn't work out,' he finished miserably.

There was a long silence and then his father said,

'I have to go back to London. Would you like to come with me?'

'No. Yes. I don't know.'

'You don't have to decide just now but I won't be spending much time here from now on. Think about it.'

They were away for a year. His father went back and forward to Newcastle and presumably stayed at the castle but he didn't ask his son to go with him and Johnny was glad he had stayed in London. He went to meetings there with his father.

His father, Johnny decided, was very clever. He didn't ever say he wanted Johnny to learn the business, but somehow information filtered through and his father would tell him what was not obvious and include him when he wanted to be included but did not seem to mind if he stayed away so that Johnny wanted to be involved.

Coming back home to Durham was strange. He had the feeling that the moment he got back somehow he and Iris would meet again and he hoped that would never happen. The wound of her turning him down had not healed.

There was always the faint hope that she had changed her mind, she had had so many months to think about it and that when he got back he might approach her again and this time she would agree. His other mind told him that she would do nothing of the sort and that he should not go back to Durham but he went anyhow.

He had been back there not more than a few days when he chanced to see Iris's brother, David, in the Garden House Hotel in North Road, sitting at the bar drinking beer and smoking with his friends. David and he were not friends and Johnny felt out of place when he went casually across and smiled and asked David how he was.

'I'm Johnny Fenwick.'

'How are you?'

The other young men there went on with their conversation and hid Johnny's words when he said,

'How's Iris?'

'She's fine.' David didn't look at him.

'She's hoping to get into the RVI in New-castle to train to become a nurse.' And then he looked at Johnny and said with a maturity Johnny was surprised at, 'I'm sorry she wouldn't marry you. That's a hard knock.'

'Thanks, it's kind of you,' Johnny said and all he wanted after that was to leave, to get out into the streets and find some air and get used to the idea that they would never be married, that Iris would follow her own ideas, she had not sat at home wishing he would come back.

He was asked to various social functions and got to know people and danced with lots of girls but he was not interested in any of them except for one poor little girl who lived on the edge of Durham polite society. He tried to ignore her but among the bright shiny girls pretending they weren't desperate for a rich husband such as he would make she stood out in some way which he could not ignore.

Pretty little Nan Fielding, she was slender and pale and there was something about her which appealed to him. He looked across the ballroom of the Waterloo Hotel in Elvet and there she was, as near to the door as she could be, as though she would have given a great deal to be somewhere else. She was wearing a white dress.

It didn't suit her. It was very old and by what he knew of such matters, which wasn't much, desperately old-fashioned, compared to dresses of the other girls who wore lovely ones with scoop necks and little sleeves which hid the tops of their arms and swinging skirts in pretty colours.

Nan's dress had a low waist and high top, floaty and little-girly. It made her face look like parchment and she was hanging about on the edge of the dance floor, twisting her hands nervously. Nobody would ask her to dance. It was well known that Nan, so strictly brought up, wouldn't even give you a kiss after the last dance.

Her mother watched closely, hawk-eyed and she had a nose like a beak. She wore black and since it was summer she looked hot and the material was faded and limp as though she had worn it a good many times before. They were poor and everybody ignored them.

Suddenly Johnny felt sorry for her and thought how brave they were to try to be part of a society that did not want them. Her father had died when Nan was small, his good name was not enough to keep them afloat here and yet they went on.

Johnny made his decision. He strode across.

'Good evening,' he said, and turned to her mother. 'Would you mind, Mrs Fielding, if I were to ask Nan to waltz?' He knew he was overdoing it but her mother wouldn't think so. Indeed, she looked startled.

'Not at all, Mr Fenwick,' she said.

'That is, if Nan would like to dance.' He looked at her.

'I would,' was all she managed and she turned enormous grey eyes on him.

She was, he thought, a terrible dancer, she trod on his toes, she turned the wrong way more than once, she was rigid, nervous, unable to concentrate on the music as though she had never danced in public and he thought it was probably true, that nobody had ever asked her and she had learned alone at home by herself in front of a mirror. Somehow it made him like her better. She did not look at him and after trying to catch her eye several times he decided to make conversation.

'So what do you like to do?' he said.

'Do?'

'Yes. Do you play tennis?'

'No. I don't know how. We have ... we have tennis courts at home but they are very overgrown.'

'I could teach you.'

'I'm not very good at things like that.'

Johnny thought of Iris swearing at him across the net at the local tennis club, doing her utmost, calling out when he was certain it was not, the arguments, the way she looked in white, the view of the hills and fields from the tennis courts, the icy cold lemonade and how he had pulled her to him and tasted the hot sweat of her neck when she had won. She had been so pleased, had loved the competition, was determined to win, to have what she wanted at all costs. It was typical of her, he decided.

Nan, he guessed, had no friends and was asked to no tennis parties. He asked her mother if they could dance again and they did. He didn't attempt to draw her near and did not think of kissing her. He was aware of people watching and of prettier more able girls than she, holding the smiles on their faces.

It was worth it, to see Nan's face transformed. She was almost beautiful then and so grateful to him. She thanked him profusely when the music ended and he asked her to dance again and he thought people would look differently at her after this and her grey eyes were lit almost like diamonds. After he had danced twice with her and deposited her back with her mother one of his friends, Bill Westwood, came over.

'You won't get anything there,' he said.

'I'm not trying to get anything,' Johnny said.

'Just as well,' Bill said.

Bill was drunk. Johnny wished he was drunk. He missed Iris so much, wanted her so badly. He didn't understand why she wouldn't marry him.

He knew suddenly that he didn't want anybody like Iris, having to have her own way, insisting on what she chose, going off to be a nurse. How stupid could you get? Nan wouldn't be like that. Nan would stay with him. She would want to be with him, he knew that she would.

He went over to where he could see that Mrs Fielding was getting ready to leave, picking up her handbag, gloves and rather dull dark coat.

'Might I come over tomorrow and take Nan out to tea?' he said.

Nan looked bewildered. So did her mother for a moment and then she looked grateful and he was sorry that she felt about things so that a simple invitation like that was so important to them.

'Mr Fenwick,' she said, 'you may,' and she swept out as best she could in her shabby array.

Johnny got home late and his father was working in the study, as he so often was late at night. He put his head round the door. His father looked up hopefully.

'Been anywhere nice?' he said.

'Dancing. I found a girl I like.'

'Good.' His father tried to hide the relief on his face and almost managed.

'She's called Nan Fielding. Have you heard of them?'

His father creased his brow.

'I think I've heard of the family. Good people.'

'Her father died a long time since and–'

'Oh, yes, they live in that broken-down house which her mother clung on to for dear life after he died. I heard about it. Why would anyone go on there with no means? It was very brave of her.'

'I'm going over tomorrow to take Nan to tea.'

'That'll be nice,' his father said.

Johnny hesitated in the doorway.

'She's the very opposite of what Iris was like.'

'I think that's good. It wouldn't do to have somebody similar. You would never be done comparing them,' his father said.

It was only when Johnny had gone that Jack felt regret. He had thought that if Johnny married Iris then at least he would see her and that because she was Johnny's wife he would learn to live without her because there was nothing less entrancing than a woman who belonged to a son you loved, he was sure.

He would be glad that they were together, he would be pleased that they were happy because he wasn't sure that Johnny would ever be really happy without her. Nan Fielding was no doubt an attractive girl and

Johnny needed somebody now but he was disappointed for his son because Johnny had needed Iris as he had needed Anna. There was also some relief in the idea that with a bit of luck he might never see Iris Black again and that Johnny would marry Nan and they would have a good marriage and he would be glad of it.

His father was right, Johnny discovered, it was as well that Iris and Nan were nothing alike and even then he found himself thinking of Iris when he went to bed, picturing in his mind how she would react when she found out that he was to be married. It made him smile.

Had she thought that he would wait for her until she finished her training or until she grew tired of nursing? How would she feel when she discovered how wrong she was? Would she come back and beg him to marry her and give Nan up? He spent several nights enjoying the idea before finally admitting to himself that Iris would do nothing of the kind but he did feel that she would be sorry and he was glad of that.

Nan was in the ladies' room at the Conservative Club and just about to leave her cubicle, come out and wash her hands when two girls burst into the otherwise empty room.

'They say he's going to marry her,' one was saying and giggling.

'You don't really think so, do you?'

'Of course not. Why on earth would somebody like Johnny Fenwick, who has everything, marry poor little Nan Fielding? She hasn't a decent rag to her back. She's wearing the same dress she wore when they met. She never wears anything else. I think it's the only dress she owns.'

Nan pressed her lips together and then she picked her evening bag from the top of the lavatory, opened the door and stepped into the room. She ignored the two girls as they fell silent. She placed the little white satin bag on the ledge above the washbasin with her gloves and, in the knowledge that they were both watching her closely, she took off the square ruby ring which Johnny had placed on her finger earlier that day.

She could see it glittering madly under the dim lights and she knew that both girls could see it too. The smell of the lavender soap was strong. She rinsed it off with warm water and then dried her hands slowly and carefully on the thin white towel. She placed the ring back on her finger, picked up her evening bag and left the room.

Outside, her eyes stung with tears. They were right of course in a sense. Johnny would never love her as he had loved Iris Black but she no longer cared. He had asked her to marry him and she had said yes and she would always remember the look of thanks on her mother's face and she would have given a great deal more to have brought happiness to the woman she loved so much.

They had nothing. Her mother had been widowed very young. Nan did not remember her father. Her mother had brought her up as best she could. Many was the night they went to bed hungry, her mother desperately keeping up appearances in the old barn of a house which she had hung on to because it was all they had, the house her father had bought for them with his last penny and a hefty mortgage.

There had been no new clothes for as long as Nan could remember. Everything was made and remade over. They had no heat except in the kitchen and although they knew it was foolish to hang on to the house they lived in the kitchen, sometimes even sleeping in there when the weather made the other rooms bitterly cold. Nan had come to love it so, it was all her mother had left of her father and they hung on to it.

Johnny Fenwick was marrying her for reasons which she could not fathom, but she didn't care. He could afford to keep her mother and her and that was all that mattered. Also, and Nan glanced down at the ring on her finger, the truth was that she adored him.

She loved him because he had saved them, because he had not gone out and married one of the other girls in the town and he could so easily have done, girls who were prettier than she was, educated and bright, daughters of university professors, business-men, doctors, or some really rich girl whom he knew in London. She could not believe that this was happening to her after years and years of poverty and loneliness. She would marry him and make him the best wife ever.

She went back into the noise of the music and there he was waiting for her, smiling.

'Would you like to dance?'

She agreed. Had his mother been small and fair-haired and agreeable? Or had she been the opposite and he wanted to move forward into something completely new? Iris Black must have been mad to turn him down was all Nan could think. What could be better than this?

He had proposed to her on the kind of relentless summer day when the shabbiness of the sitting-room furniture showed up so that she would have preferred to close the curtains, except that there was no point since there was nothing left to spoil. The curtains were practically in shreds. Her mother would not have new ones because they had been good and she could afford only cheap material. They had wonderful birds on them, oriental with long tails. Silk curtains. Whoever could afford such things now? And they were still beautiful in their way.

The chairs were orangey red and threadbare where once they had been dark coloured. The carpet was dulled and thin. The piano keys were yellow and some of them – the ivory having cracked and broken – did not play at all, no matter how softly she tried. Beyond the window the lawn was high, the beds were full of weeds. She and her mother concentrated on vegetables so the front garden had not been well tended for many a year.

In the orchard the plum, pear and apple trees were so old that their barks split and a year or two ago when it had been a fruitful autumn – she remembered very well how the wasps had stung her again and again as she gathered the fruit for bottling and preserving against the winter – many of the branches weighed down by fruit had fractured and broken. Some of them did not have fruit to offer any more. Rather like her mother they had given everything they could and were worn out.

She could not understand what Johnny was doing there. He had taken her to the pictures, they had danced together twice at local dances and he had come to the house for tea. It was more than any other man had done, but she did not expect him to stand awkwardly by the door when she could hear the cathedral bells chiming four o'clock and ask her to many him. It was not that she thought she had misheard, it was just that she had not expected the words.

'I want to marry you, Nan.'

He said it so quickly as though he did not want to say it, or wanted to get past the declaration as soon as possible.

'Do you like me at all?' he said next and that was even more surprising.

He wanted her to like him?

'Yes, of course.' She was almost stuttering.

'Of course?' He seemed perplexed.

She couldn't tell him that nobody had ever paid her any attention, that she did not think herself pretty, that she had no clothes to show off her slender figure, no father in the small society of the stuffy little city to further her interests. She was nobody and nothing.

'Why?' she said.

'Why what?'

'Why should you want to marry me?'

'I would like to look after you.'

Nan smiled. The smile, she could feel it, got broader and broader.

'What a lovely sentiment,' she said and then hesitated.

'What is it?' he said.

'Why should you want me after...'

'After Iris Black?' he completed the sentence for her. 'It wouldn't have worked. Iris didn't want marriage, I don't think she would ever have wanted it, whereas I do, I want somebody all to myself and I find you very appealing. Do you like me, Nan?'

It was the second time he had asked so he really wanted to know. She would have said yes to any man who could look after them. She could not believe she had landed what was the biggest marital prize in the area. Such things had never happened to her before.

'No,' she said, 'I'm after your money,' and when he laughed she realized she had managed to make a joke because it was true and yet it was not and she was honest and yet she could not bear to tell him how she wondered what she would feel like in his arms. No man had ever touched her and now ... she wanted to shout and shriek and be wild for the first time ever. She wanted him to make mad passionate love to her. She didn't know whether she could keep her hands off him for another second.

'There is just one thing,' she said.

He looked worried.

'What is it?' he said.

'Would you kiss me?'

He looked startled. Maybe women weren't supposed to say such things to men who had just proposed, perhaps they were meant to sit there and wait until he suggested or did such a thing. Whatever, he came across and took her into his arms and kissed her as she was convinced nobody had ever been kissed before in the history of time.

It was wonderful and she returned it, got her hands up around his neck and into his hair and when he might have stopped for respectability's sake she held him close and encouraged him and even as he let go she looked into his eyes and felt transformed.

'Oh,' she said with a little sigh, 'that was even better than I imagined and I didn't think it was possible that it could be.'

He laughed, looked surprised but pleased.

'I want you to be my wife, Nan, and you need never again be jealous of anybody because I will be good to you, I promise. Do you want me to ask your mother for your hand?'

'Could we ask her together?' Nan said. 'She'll be so pleased and I want to see her face.'

'There is one thing,' he said.

Nan stopped, already worrying.

'I wondered if your mother would like us to move in with her? I don't want to live with my father, he's hardly ever there. He certainly doesn't want to live with me and your house is enormous. Of course if you would like we could buy somewhere new but I thought your mother would miss you since there's only the two of you. I will have to go to London sometimes on business with my father but you won't mind that if you have your mother to keep you company and you could both come too and do lots of shopping. That would be nice for your mother.'

Nan didn't like to say, 'She has no money,' and then she thought it would not be true for much longer, they would have plenty of money. Whatever had she done that a man like this should rescue her? It didn't happen in real life.

Maidens in towers withered and died in them, she thought. Nobody ever came to their rescue. Only people who didn't need rescuing, like Iris Black, were loved by men like this but perhaps in time, if she was the best wife ever, he would learn to love her. In the meanwhile she would settle for whatever he was willing to give her and it was already much more than she had ever hoped for.

'The house is dropping to pieces but I would be loath to leave it,' she said.

'You and your mother could make changes if you like after the wedding.'

It was the proudest day of Nan's life when he asked her mother for her hand, and when her mother had bestowed it on him, whether they could live with her.

When it was late and he had gone home Nan went upstairs to her mother's big shabby bedroom where nothing had been altered for as long as she could remember. Her mother was standing by the open window, looking out over two acres of wilderness.

'Perhaps we'll be able to have a gardener,' Nan ventured as she drew nearer.

Her mother turned and kissed her and in the last rays of the summer sunshine she looked years younger than she had looked before the proposal.

'You aren't just doing this for the money, are you?' she said.

'And if I were?'

Her mother sighed.

'Men are difficult enough creatures even when you love them.'

'I expect we are too.'

'They are obsessed with stupid things, football, shooting, beer.'

'Whereas we like real things – bracelets, shoes, lipstick.'

They laughed.

'We might even be able to afford those things,' Nan said.

Her mother didn't say anything and was unusually quiet when something so momentous had happened.

'Don't you want me to marry him?' Nan said.

'I don't want you to marry him for his money. I know we need it badly but I married your father because I wanted him. I didn't regret it for a second even though we had so little time together. I adored him.

Don't marry Mr Fenwick for the wrong reasons. We'll get by, we always have done.'

Nan thought it was the bravest speech she had ever heard and made her smile.

'Oh, Mother,' she said, 'he kissed me and it was the most divine thing that ever happened,' and they both laughed.

'Just think,' her mother said, 'if you were to have a child.'

'Just think,' Nan said, 'if he bought me a ruby.'

And he had.

Five

Her mother was big with news, Iris could see, the moment she turned around in the silence which followed her mother's entrance into the room and still her mother looked at her.

'What is it?' Iris's heart began to beat fast. 'Has something awful happened?'

'No, no.' Her mother spoke quickly to be reassuring but her hands almost fluttered in agitation. 'It's just that Johnny Fenwick is engaged to be married.' The last seven words came out in a rush. Iris heard them over and over in her head.

'Oh,' she said with a lightness which was false but not wanting her mother to know it, 'and who's the lucky lady?'

'Nan Fielding.'

Iris wanted to toss her head and say that she didn't care but her mother would know it was not true, and she did not want her mother to be distressed. Her parents, though they had said nothing, were disappointed she had chosen not to marry him, she knew. It was not fair to burden her mother further.

'I see.'

'Do you wish you had chosen differently?'

her mother said and when Iris shook her head her mother looked relieved.

'And it was the truth,' she said to David late that evening.

It was her favourite time of day. Her parents had gone to bed. She and David were sitting in the garden. He was home from university and she had a rare day off from the hospital.

'Yes,' he said as they sat watching the sun set and they both smoked a final cigarette, 'but wouldn't it be nice not to have to make choices like that? You always end up having to sacrifice something. Nan is the very opposite of you.'

Iris had come to the same conclusion.

'Yes, she's biddable, domesticated, probably wants heaps of babies and will be there for him with a nice dinner on the table when he comes home from work in the evenings.'

'Sounds good,' David said, 'but very dull,' and he grinned.

He always managed to make her feel better.

'It was the haste with which he did it that surprised me,' Iris said, 'as though anybody would do.'

'It isn't so long since his mother died.'

'Lord,' Iris said, stretching out her legs in front of her, 'I don't think I want to be a substitute for anybody's mother,' and they both laughed.

It was not true of course, she thought when she went to bed. He had done it out of resentment, out of spite if Johnny could be spiteful, and she was not sure that he could. He had loved her and hated that she had not wanted what he had wanted, that was all.

It was a raw deal for Nan but then it was difficult to feel sorry for the woman who would be the partner to Johnny's love-making, who would go to sleep and wake up with him, have sons and daughters with his beautiful eyes, make a home with him and... There she stopped. There was time enough for such things and if Johnny could not see it then it was no good.

She did not regret her decision. She regretted sleeping alone. She thought back to the wonderful afternoons and evenings in bed with him, the summer days with the sun's warmth coming in beyond the half-closed curtains, the sweat on his back, the salt on his mouth, the way that their bodies fitted together so perfectly, the apparently endless times in bed with him, that perfection of his lovemaking.

She had thought it would go on and on. They were so young. Perhaps it was because of his mother dying, though it seemed simplistic indeed to explain it so. Yet she understood that he should try to recreate the apparent perfection of his parents' marriage. Why should he not want to see that again?

She knew that it was wonderful to come home to someone but she wanted more – noise, movement, music, novelty, exciting places, people she did not yet know. Was Johnny really prepared to give all that up for meat and two veg and the reassurance of marriage? She thought it small of him and then she relented.

If it was what he wanted then she hoped he would be happy and poor little Nan – it made Iris smile to think of all the girls who must be livid with envy and fury that Nan had caught Johnny Fenwick.

She hoped Nan would make him a wonderful wife and give him half a dozen children if they wanted them and that he would buy her wonderful jewellery and lots of furs so that she could go swanning about town as she had never been able to and that people who had once barely spoken to her would feel obliged to be nice.

When Iris had become certain she wanted to train to be a nurse she had written to the matron at the Royal Victoria Infirmary with an application to become a student nurse and was aware that it was difficult to be accepted and would take time.

She had never been very good at school, had not thought much about it, but she did now and wished that she had tried harder. She had no experience and did not know where the desire for nursing had come from. Her mother had always been hopeless with such things and could not bear it when they were ill.

On the morning that she found on the hall mat a letter which she was certain was the letter telling her she had been turned down she opened the envelope with shaking hands.

Luckily nobody else was about but she opened it as fast as she could, thinking if it was bad news at least she would learn of it by herself. She spread open the letter and realized her mother was standing at the far end of the hall beside the kitchen, waiting and hoping ... for what?

'I've been accepted for interview.'

Her mother's face cleared, not completely but mostly, glad, Iris knew, that she had accomplished the first thing she had tried for but anxious as to the future. She came down and hugged her.

'I'm so pleased for you,' she said.

It was just the beginning. Iris got off the train in Newcastle on the appointed day and was trembling and felt sick. The feelings increased as she reached the hospital, in the town.

It did not look like anywhere she might be able to go. It looked so forbidding there amidst the rest of the city. She wished that she had stayed at home, though what she would have done there she could not think and she knew that she had been bored for so long, feeling that she had no place.

Her friends were getting married, they all had young men. Iris felt so out of things, she was looking for a place in life and if it was not here then where would it be?

She found the matron in her private office. Iris thought she was the most frightening person she had ever seen, tiny with a long thin nose and bright shrewd eyes. Her voice had a staccato quality which it would take somebody very brave to contradict. Iris was convinced that nobody must ever be able to speak in her presence but somehow she found a voice when the questions were rapped out at her, all about her home life, her parents, her schooling and why she wanted to become a nurse.

She had tried to think of why but the truth was she had no idea. She certainly had no Florence Nightingale ideas about it, no vision of healing, no spectacular idea of ministering to the sick, just a practicality which she was sure of.

She tried to express herself as best she could only to be told that she had not distinguished herself at school and did not seem to know what she was doing there. Iris trembled.

Dismissed with barely a civil word she found herself almost in tears when she got outside and wishing she had said more, that she had answered differently. She went home very cast down and thankfully David was driving down the street just beyond the station.

'I didn't know you were going to be here,' she said, 'I'm so glad you came back and I caught you. I think I made a complete mess of it.'

'I had a couple of days free and came back specially. Get in,' he said.

'What?'

'Well, nobody knows you're back yet.'

He drove to the Three Tuns Hotel in New Elvet and ordered tea and cakes.

'I should have gone home. They'll be anxious as to how it went,' she said.

'Tell me about it.'

So she did.

'It doesn't sound to me as though it was that bad. I think you're worrying too much.'

'What if I don't get in?'

'There are other nursing schools,' David said and she hadn't thought of that, hadn't considered it and she brightened up and ate two pieces of angel cake and had two cups of tea before he drove her back to the house.

'I'm so glad you came home. Thank you for that,' she said as she got out as her mother, hearing the car, came rushing out to see them.

Her mother sat them down and gave them

tea – again – and Iris went over the interview and then her father came in and she was obliged to go through it yet again. Afterwards they had dinner and then she and David went into town and to a little pub called the Three Hearts of Gold in Church Street, opposite to St Oswald's Church which Iris had always thought the perfect name for a pub, and they had whisky and a couple of cigarettes, and by then Iris was past caring whether she got into the RVI, she was glad she had done it but she decided that she wouldn't worry about it.

She began worrying the very next day and went on for several days until finally the letter came and she had been offered a place as a probationer.

'I'm going, I'm going,' she shrieked at her mother and it was Saturday so they were there to read the letter and to wish her well and that was when she became terrified and wanted to change her mind.

That summer was rather like the summer had been before David went to boarding school, she felt as though it would be the last summer they would ever spend together.

They played a lot of tennis, they went to parties where people danced all night and drank lurid cocktails. Iris danced with lots of different men but to her they were all just not Johnny Fenwick. She did not let any of them go so far as to kiss her. She never saw him. It was as though he had disappeared off the face of the earth and when she mentioned it to one friend, Thelma Peters, Thelma said,

'I thought you knew. They spend a lot of time in London. I understand his father has a house there and he's in business with his father and is doing very well, making a great deal of money. Don't you wish you'd married him now?'

'Not at all,' Iris said, 'I don't want to marry anybody.'

'I can't think why you want to be a nurse. The whole thing sounds disgusting to me,' Thelma said and although Iris was sure she was right she did not agree.

Six

There was not a single time during the hard months that followed during which Iris wished she had married Johnny Fenwick and that was strange to her because her life at the RVI was unadulterated hell. There was nothing but work and sleep.

It felt right as nothing before had done. It was not that she was happy, it was just that her whole existence felt right.

The room where she lived was small. There were three single beds in it with a tiny space between them. Rickety wardrobes stood at the end and there was a chest of drawers. Iris tried to comfort herself that she was a short train journey from home but it seemed so much further away.

She was just beginning to feel extremely homesick on the first day when the door opened and two young women of about her own age came in. One was very pretty with red hair and dark eyes, the other though similar-looking was much bigger and not pretty at all.

'I'm Joyce Dobson,' the first girl said.

'And I'm her elder sister, Wilhelmina, and I know it's a stupid name so everybody just calls me Wilkie.'

Iris introduced herself and was so glad to have found somebody friendly to share with.

The nursing school was very like Iris had always thought boarding school would be which was one of the reasons she had never wanted to go to such a place. It could not have been any worse.

They were told what to do, when to sleep, when to eat, when to go out – almost never. They were not allowed to talk, they had to bow their heads for grace before meals, the food was inedible, she lost a lot of weight during the first three months and on several occasions almost walked out.

Many girls couldn't stand it and left and that was one reason Iris could not go. She knew that in their hearts her parents had not wanted her to do this and she was not now going to go and tell them that she had changed her mind because it was too hard. She thought she understood why it was too hard and that frightened her, the responsibility, the stamina needed, the mindless obedience necessary when things went wrong.

Being in the army was probably similar, she thought, and if other people could stand it so could she. Also she knew that Joyce and Wilkie had come from a much harder life than she had.

They lived at Heath Houses, which was a mining village just outside Durham and not more than a mile or so from where Iris lived, but she learned from them that it was very different.

Their mother kept a small shop in the back room of their house. Their father had been injured in the pit and no longer worked but their parents were proud of them for getting so far and they did not think that being here was hard, which made Iris ashamed for being so well off. She did not dare to complain even though often she was so tired that she could barely think.

They worked six days a week and on their days off did nothing other than sleep and they had to study all the time. Strangely she found the studying easy, she who had been no good at school, but this time it was a subject she had some enthusiasm for.

That had not happened before and it made a lot of difference. She was proud of the fact that people would come to her room and ask her things they had not understood and she tried to explain simply to them.

The money she made was so little that it made her laugh to think of it but then she did not need it like the others, her parents had always kept her and the money that she did make lay in her bank account accumulating interest.

Joyce and Wilkie's money was for their

parents, they had not a penny. It made things difficult because she would have liked to help them out. In fact, she thought, all she could do without seeming patronizing was to take them out to tea when they were off together and it happened so infrequently that it didn't look bad.

They both protested but Iris excused herself by being brisk and saying they were not to argue because it was the one time they could be together in any degree of comfort so in the little time they had free they found a wonderful teashop in town and stuffed themselves with sandwiches, cakes and hot tea and she was happy to pay.

Her mother, presumably remembering David's days at boarding school, often sent them food parcels and they scoffed chocolate cake after lights out just as though they were in the dorm. Wilkie snored but the others were too tired to care. They always slept well.

The first year ended with examinations and they all passed, and after that they went into what Iris thought of as real nursing and for the first time they worked in the wards on night duty and it was the hardest thing she had ever done.

Even Wilkie, who seemed to have more energy than the rest, did nothing but sleep in her time off. They worked for three weeks solid and then had three days and Iris kept promising herself that she would go home but she didn't manage it, she was too exhausted.

Every time she told herself it could not get any more difficult or any more strenuous it did but she began to get the hang of being always tired and always worried about lectures and falling asleep and that she might inadvertently kill one of the patients. She began to get used to the whole thing and she discovered that it was what she had wanted. Why anybody could want anything like that she had no idea but it was her whole life now.

During the next two years they worked in the wards, giving the qualified nurses time off. It was scary, especially at night. Why did more people become ill at night? she wondered. There were a lot more crises on night shift and she dreaded the responsibility at first but she discovered that you grew used to anything if you did it often enough. There were night rounds by the doctors and sometimes they could last a long time and there was always the telephone if there was an emergency.

Four o'clock in the morning was the hardest time. It took many months to learn not to want to go to sleep then and why it was harder than three o'clock Iris did not know, as though a natural time came when everyone ought to be in bed and those who were not found it the worst time for people becoming more ill or dying.

Time off was precious and was for sleeping and Iris was always so relieved when her stint of night shift was over.

During the final year one night when she had gone happily to bed in the knowledge that she would have a full eight hours which she so badly needed she thought she was in the middle of a nightmare. Somebody was calling her name and nudging her most unkindly, like an elbow in the ribs. She protested and tried to turn over and the voice and the nudging became more heavy.

Soon sufficiently awake to realize something was going on, Iris stirred. She leant on one elbow, unaware at first of what had disturbed her. A figure was sitting on the bottom of her bed.

After several seconds of panic she put out a hand to the little lamp which sat on the bedside table. Cream light showed her Joyce, white-faced. She was not crying but she had been. Her eyes were narrowed from tears and looked sore, so it was not a small problem, Iris surmised as she willed herself up from the depths of heavy sleep. Wilkie was on night shift, it was just the two of them.

'Whatever is it?' she said irritably because to Joyce everything was a problem, she was forever having what she considered to be a crisis when it was something everybody else took for granted. Surely it could not warrant Joyce waking her up when she was so tired.

In answer Joyce put a handkerchief to her face and shook her head.

'I'm awake now,' Iris said, yawning, 'whatever it is spit it out and then let me go back to sleep. I'm exhausted.'

'I'm expecting a baby,' Joyce said.

Iris sat up even further. She had realized weeks ago that something was wrong but since Joyce had not chosen to confide in her she did not like to ask. This was indeed a crisis. She sighed inwardly, thinking how typical it was of Joyce to get herself into something so awkward and then get other people involved too. Sometimes she wished they were not friends, Joyce was so troublesome.

'Are you sure?' she said.

Joyce looked at her with a hint of impatience.

'It could be something else,' Iris suggested. 'A stomach upset, too much work and worry to stop your periods—'

Joyce's face crumpled into misery.

'It isn't,' she said, 'I didn't want to tell anybody but I have to and I don't want to tell Wilkie, she'll be cross and my mam and dad would be so ashamed of me and...' She gave way to sobs.

'How far on are you?'

'What does that have to do with it?' Joyce

said, searching in vain for a dry handkerchief in her pocket.

'There are ways round it, you know,' Iris
said, 'if you're less than three months or so.'

Joyce stared, wet eyes getting bigger and
bigger.

'Do you mean...?'

'Do you want it?'

'Of course I don't want it, do you think
I'm mad, but we can't do anything like that,
you would get thrown out of here and Wilkie
would never stand for it.'

'It's not my life or hers, it's yours,' Iris
said.

'I did it. I can't just go and ... undo it like
that.'

'Whose is it?'

Joyce looked stubborn.

'Is it George's?'

George Bell was the local curate and Iris
knew Joyce had seen him once or twice.

'No, of course not.'

'Why of course not? You did sleep with
him, didn't you?'

Joyce didn't reply.

'Who then? Not that stupid boy–'

'I think it's Melvyn's.'

Iris screwed up her eyes, trying to see
Joyce's face better in the semi-darkness.

'Melvyn?' Iris couldn't believe it. Was Joyce
desperate? 'Do you want to marry him?'

'It isn't as simple as that.'

'Why not? What do you mean?'

'Melvyn is married.'

Her voice was flat, devoid of any emotion other than weariness.

Iris stared into the little pool of light which the lamp gave. She hadn't liked Melvyn from the beginning.

How Joyce had had the energy to find somebody to go out with when they never stopped working and studying Iris couldn't think and she didn't like to say so, but on their few days off when had Joyce found the time to sleep with Melvyn, who worked at Martins Bank in Gateshead and had met Joyce in a local pub one night?

She had been late back on more than one occasion and Iris had been worried that she would be caught and dismissed. Iris couldn't think of anybody wanting to marry Melvyn, who was shorter than George, skinny and sour-faced with no discernible intelligence.

'Are you sure?'

Joyce raised her eyes.

'He told me he was and that's enough, surely.'

Iris stopped herself from saying, 'Who in their right minds would marry that little toad?' and tried to think, and after she had thought she said, 'Did you tell him about the baby?'

'Of course I did.'

'And you don't think he just wants to get

away with it?'

'I love him, Iris.'

'Don't be ridiculous,' Iris said, before she could stop herself. Really, Joyce had no brains at all. Love was nothing to do with sleeping together before marriage otherwise she and Johnny Fenwick would have been dashing down the aisle. 'What about George?'

Joyce looked confused.

'George is a vicar, well, a curate at the moment but he will be a vicar,' Joyce said as though this put George quite out of the question. 'I did sleep with him once. Once was enough. He was so sorry afterwards. I suppose being religious gets you like that.'

'That's the answer,' Iris said, 'you can marry him.'

'I can't possibly.'

'Then what are you going to do, tell your parents?'

Joyce looked horrified.

'Get rid of it?'

Joyce looked even more shocked.

'Tell me one sensible alternative that you've come up with.'

'I haven't had time to come up with anything. I just assumed Melvyn would marry me.'

'I think in the long run you'll be glad you didn't.'

'And in the long run I'll be glad I didn't

marry George. I can try drinking a bottle of gin.'

'Or stick a knitting needle up yourself?' Iris said tartly. The tears were welling again. 'Could you bring up a child on your own?'

'Of course not. I couldn't hurt my mam and dad like that.'

'George is the only person you can marry, unless you've been sleeping with other people.' She glanced at Joyce's hurt face. 'He'll have a job and a house. What more could you ask? He has to do the right thing, otherwise his bishop will find out and he'll be defrocked or whatever they call it. I'm sure that vicars are supposed to marry.'

'Not in a hurry.'

'I doubt he'll be the first,' Iris said.

George had asked Iris to go out with him. Iris hadn't liked to tell Joyce when Joyce first started seeing him. Now it was difficult not to wish that she had told her but Joyce seemed to like him at first and they had so little time off and Joyce had not had an easy life before she met him. She had dreamed of them being happy together. How stupid it seemed now. And also she had been glad when Joyce met George because Joyce had said, 'George is a big step up, you know,' and then she had seen him once and twice and never again and Iris didn't know whether to be glad or happy about it.

George seemed posh to Joyce. She liked

his accent, she thought it made her look good to be seen with him. Wilkie had never liked him.

'How on earth will you tell your sister?' she said now.

Joyce looked horrified. 'I can't.'

'She'll find out, so the sooner you tell her the better.'

'Will you come with me when I tell George?'

'Are you really going to deceive him?'

'What else can I do? You're right,' Joyce said.

Seven

Standing in the cold on the corner of Northumberland Street, one of the lovely stone streets in the centre of Newcastle, while Joyce sat in the gloomy little cafe in a side street just beyond and talked to George, Iris felt guilty, responsible. Should she have urged Joyce to marry a man who had possibly not got her pregnant? But then what alternative was there?

Besides, George had not thought of what damage he might do and she comforted herself with the idea that Joyce was stupid enough not to be sure which man she was pregnant by, even though she was a nurse. Nurses, Iris thought cynically, were the worst offenders of such things, as though knowledge made them immune.

She could see George's face, because they had chosen a seat by the window, and he was what her mother called 'ashen'. He had had a shock. Was he going to marry her? It was difficult to tell.

Iris didn't like to stare, she had spent most of the last hour with her back turned but kept sneaking looks at them as best she could. The waitress had deposited tea and some unappetizing grey cakes on the table and as far as Iris could judge neither had touched the other person.

They sat at opposite sides of the table as though they were going into battle and it might well be true. Iris tried to think of all the possibilities so that she should be armed before they came outside, ready to say whatever was necessary to get George to marry Joyce, but if he could not be moved, if he would not admit to responsibility for the child it was difficult to know what to do and then ... she did not want to think about Joyce as an unmarried mother, having to go back to Heath Houses and tell her parents, because Iris would have to go with her.

What if they should throw her out? She didn't think they would, they were such good people, but it would be very shameful and what would happen to Joyce if she could not live at her home any more? What would she do?

Iris wanted to panic and run away, pretend it was nothing to do with her, and although she told herself several times during the hour or so they were inside that everything was going to be all right she could not convince herself that she would not end up having to take Joyce back home with her to her parents and then there would be explanations all over again and...

Finally they came into the street and George turned to face Joyce as they did so and he was shaking his head and his eyes were narrowed, small, resentful and harder than Iris had noticed them being before, almost piggy eyes she thought uncharitably and then with a shudder thanked God that she hadn't slept with him.

'I don't believe this is anything to do with me and I won't have anything more to do with it or you.'

He was ready to abandon Joyce there on the street. Iris could see that flight was the only thing on George's mind, he wanted to get away, to get rid of the unwanted responsibility, of a future full of Joyce and her swelling abdomen.

She didn't blame him for that in a way, it was the thing many people would have done. Joyce was so unreliable, maybe George suspected her of sleeping with somebody else or that it was unlikely a child had been conceived from one night or possibly two's whatever-you-called-it in these circumstances.

There was something in her which made her pity him for all his carelessness. Men thought about nothing but sex so it was difficult to blame George for one slip. Some bastards did it all the time and probably many of them got away with it. He was unlucky and worse still, she could see that he felt guilty because of who he was or because of God. She didn't imagine he had gone to bed with many people or possibly with anybody else, he wasn't the most attractive man in the world, clergymen weren't. He was short and stout, what the tailors called 'portly' with a belly and a double chin, and he was going bald already. He would have made a good Friar Tuck, Iris thought.

Nevertheless he had to take responsibility for this, there was nobody else and Iris could see that Joyce was already doubting the outcome of this meeting. She could not go back to that little pit row an unmarried mother. Iris wanted to shake her but that would have been pointless.

'George–' Joyce pleaded.

George turned away but by then Iris was there and he was facing her. She looked him straight in the eyes. She had to do this or George would get away and everything would be lost. She couldn't let him walk off, even if he went down the street with her dragging on to the sleeve of his coat.

'If your bishop finds out you'll be in trouble,' she said.

'How would he find out, unless you are suggesting to me that you would tell him?'

'Joyce will be kicked out of the nursing school. She can hardly go home to her parents with a baby. Her father was badly hurt down the pit and can't work. Her mother runs a shop in her back room to keep them.'

'She should have thought of that,' George said.

'You should have thought of it.'

George was so white he was almost grey, and angry. Iris was rather afraid that George cared nothing that they were in broad daylight on Northumberland Street and that people were aware of the scene they were causing.

'You're supposed to be better than the rest of us,' Iris pointed out.

'That's not what being ordained is all about,' George said with slight humour. 'You don't know the first thing about the Church, Iris.'

'I know they wouldn't like to hear that you are about to become a father and are shirking the responsibility,' she said, glad that he could see anything funny about this situation and that he was obviously wavering.

Joyce was very pretty and rather silly and most men seemed to prefer that to sensible women, maybe because the pretty vacant ones like Joyce were more inclined to sleep with them and damn the consequences. Opportunity egged men on to pretty girls.

George looked at her with reluctant admiration.

'Thank you, Iris, you're such a help,' he said.

Iris stood against the bitter wind which whipped up Northumberland Street and she looked him in the eye.

'You will marry her, then?'

George didn't answer.

'There is no way round this,' Iris said.

'If you fail your exams I should think blackmail would be a decent career for you,' George said.

Iris wanted to leave but she stood her ground.

'It's a baby, George. Your son.' It had been the right thing to say, she could see. What man could resist the idea of a son? They were all such egotistical idiots. And that was what finished him off in the end. Iris could not help but hope savagely that Joyce gave him half a dozen girls in the time they were married.

After the interview – why did she think of it like that, she wondered – when George had said he would sort everything out – Iris doubted he would and was prepared to do so if he did not – she remembered his eyes so full of bitterness. When he had gone and Joyce had cried against the kind of wind which would dry your eyes in seconds, Iris wondered what kind of stupid deity was so keen on ensuring the preservation of the species that people went around indiscriminately reproducing like bloody rabbits, thereby blighting their whole lives.

Contraception was the answer to almost

all the problems women had, she thought. Decent contraception would give them power. Why didn't they have it now? Condoms were all right but they didn't always work, men wouldn't always wear them and they stank. Women needed to control these things, they really did, she thought.

She put an arm around Joyce and walked her away from the town and back to the hospital, and once in their room she brought out of her hiding place a bottle of brandy, put a large amount into a cup and gave it to her and when Joyce had stopped crying and snivelling Iris said, 'You must tell Wilkie.' She wished very much that Joyce had told her sister before now.

Braver for the brandy, Joyce nodded her head. 'All right,' she said.

In their room later Iris sat while Joyce told her sister, and Wilkie was too intelligent not to know that Iris had been her sister's confidante but she said nothing, she only looked across levelly at Iris while Joyce explained that George was the father of her child and they were to be married.

'You've seen him, then?'

'Yes.' Joyce didn't look up.

Later, when Joyce slept, exhausted by the ordeal, her pregnancy and no doubt the brandy, Iris and Wilkie smoked. They were not meant to do so in their room and neither, she imagined, were they meant to drink. Nobody would think of the nurses doing such a thing. They sat on Wilkie's bed with their cups and the comforting brown liquid and Wilkie glanced down at her sleeping sister and said,

'Thank you, Iris, you're a good lass.'

Iris feigned surprise.

'I didn't do anything.'

Wilkie looked at her.

'You didn't have to pay him or blackmail him?'

Wilkie, Iris decided, was too clever.

'The stupid thing is I envy her,' Wilkie said.

'Oh, Wilkes, you shouldn't.' Usually Wilkie was pleased at this affectionate shortening of her shortened name and even now she smiled.

'No lad ever wanted me,' she said. 'Even Billy from down the row who was boz-eyed and slow never asked me to go down the alley with him.'

Iris laughed and dragged on her cigarette and put it burning on the edge of the saucer they were using as an ashtray before pouring more brandy into their cups.

'If he'd asked our bloody Joyce she would have,' Wilkie observed, sharp through the drink. 'How many men has she had?'

'Two, I think, up to now.'

'Melvyn and George? I think I might have

been better off with Billy the Boz-Eyed. What about you?'

Iris considered her brandy.

'Only Johnny.'

'Do you wish that you had married him?'

'No. I'd rather be here. Do you think that's awful?'

'I think choice is the important thing,' Wilkie said. 'Me, I'd like a nice man. I'd like somebody tall and lean with beautiful muscle tone,' she said and laughed at herself. 'Men like that are usually stupid but I don't think I would care. I would like to have somebody make passionate love to me. How daft am I? Do you think anybody will ever want me, Iris?'

'Of course they will. They would be mad not to.'

'I'm plain and fat and sharp-tongued.'

'It doesn't stop most women,' Iris said and they giggled and she poured some more brandy. 'I'm skinny and horrible.'

'You are,' her friend agreed. She sat back against the wall behind her bed and sighed. 'This is right, though. I never used to think I'd have something that meant so much.'

'Neither did I. We're lucky.'

'I don't know that Joyce is going to be very lucky,' Wilkie said. 'That George, I think he's mean and ... did you ever notice that he has small eyes? However will we tell Mam and Dad?'

'Don't tell them. We can arrange the marriage very fast and the baby will be premature.'

'I think my mam is too bright not to work it out.'

'But for your dad's sake she won't,' Iris said.

Iris and Wilkie were bridesmaids. Iris's mother made a white dress for Joyce and two blue matching dresses for Iris and Wilkie and their garden provided pink and white roses for the bouquet and if anybody thought the wedding rushed they had the sense not to say so.

Joyce and George were married in the little parish church at Heath Houses and had the reception in the church hall. Iris had confided to her mother that Joyce was pregnant and her mother had insisted on contributing a great deal to the food and her father had bought the sherry. They had managed to do this while not offending Joyce's parents.

'You bought them,' Iris said to George, 'nobody will know.'

'You're the soul of tact.'

'I just want to get through this without anybody being hurt any further,' Iris said. 'Her parents can't afford it and God knows you haven't done much so far other than the obvious. Try to look as though you aren't going to the scaffold.'

It was the morning of the wedding and George looked ill.

'You haven't got morning sickness, have you, George?' Iris said.

The look he threw her would have halted an incoming tide.

As Iris stood in the church with the rain pouring down and the wind throwing it in great waves against the windows she thought how very lucky she was not to be Joyce, not obliged to marry some stuffed shirt like George, who thought he was everybody's intellectual superior and had all the sensitivity of a paving stone.

And she thanked God that she had had Johnny Fenwick and not become pregnant and loved him and enjoyed his body and got away scot-free, except that it wasn't because in some ways she would never cease to want him.

Compared to Joyce's fate however she felt free, light, glad, very pleased that it was nothing to do with her. Her parents and David were both there and her mother wore a lovely hat with a feather and David and her father wore smart suits.

George and Joyce went off to Scarborough for the weekend and she and David and her parents went back to their house and Wilkie stayed in Heath Houses with her parents.

Iris slept most of the next day, punctuated by a huge breakfast, an even bigger dinner at midday and her mother piling food into a bag. David collected Wilkie and they both got on the train. Wilkie looked happily at the bag.

'Chocolate cake?' she said hopefully and somehow that was when Iris realized how much Wilkie was already missing her sister. She would miss Joyce too. Things would not be the same without her.

'Will we be all right?' she asked.

'She would have made a good nurse,' Wilkie said with regret.

Nobody was moved into their room because they were only months away from their final exams. Iris was pleased to get the whole thing over with but in a stupid kind of way she didn't want to leave and go on to the next part of her life because she had grown used to being in Newcastle and the nursing.

The examinations were hard and felt as though they were going on forever and then suddenly they were all over and it was the late spring and Iris was leaving the RVI for the last time, the little room where she and Joyce and Wilkie had become such friends and all the other girls she had met who now mattered to her.

She didn't want to go home, she didn't want to leave what had become familiar and secure. She didn't regret a single second of it, she was just worried that one of them would get through and one of them wouldn't, which was worse than them both failing.

There was also Hitler to be considered. If there was to be a war Iris was aware that nurses would be needed and also that inexperienced nurses would be left behind to cope here, and she thought that if she was to put her skills to good use she would want to do it abroad, where the fighting was going on.

She was not sure whether the people in charge of such things would agree with her, she was quite certain that her parents would not but when she and Wilkie talked about it they thought that if they passed their exams and had a little time nursing here they would, when the war was certain, try to join the Queen Alexandra nurses.

Even the sound of it was exciting, she thought, to say nothing of the wonderful grey and scarlet uniforms and the tradition of brilliant nursing. It became her ambition to serve in this way. Women would be needed in all kinds of professions and hers would be one of the most necessary.

In time they both had letters from the General Nursing Council for England and Wales. They had passed their examinations. They were now officially SRNs. It was the proudest moment of Iris's life. She didn't care what she had given up or sacrificed for it. This was her whole life now.

Eight

George Bell was not a bad man, at least Joyce didn't think so. He was just a man who had been paid out a thousandfold for a stupid moment of indulgence and they were both paying the price. George was given a parish in the dockland of Newcastle.

'For you,' he said, with obvious bitterness, 'it should be just like home.'

They had a house which was the very opposite of the houses most vicars' wives endured, it stood in a busy street, something new for Joyce.

The little pit village she came from was small and grimy and the pitmen came home black from the pit but the people were friendly. It was a place where everybody knew one another and the pit wives mostly prided themselves on keeping their houses clean, but the dirt around the dockside in Newcastle was endless years of wet fish and stinking alleys and houses which had rotten windows and tumble-down walls, all huddled together in dark, narrow streets.

Thin, badly shod children roamed the area and there were men from ships from all over the world. Foreign accents disrupted day and night, loud and drunk. The place was full of singing, men throwing up as they rid themselves of their pay when they came off the ships and into the many pubs. Pockets were thieved, fat prostitutes propped up the street corners and from the pubs came the smell of fried food and burned oil, cigarettes, pipes and a hundred seafaring shanties.

Joyce was appalled. She did not understand the local accents. The people here talked so fast that often she wrongly assumed they were from Sweden or Norway. The house itself was damp and smelled sweetly of mice. Long-tailed rats slunk into dark corners in the half light of evening outside her door.

There was undoubtedly, Joyce thought, plenty of the work that vicars should be doing but it was difficult not to feel a little sorry for George who, she thought, though he didn't voice his frustrated hopes, had envisaged taking tea with elderly spinsters and looking out from his study at fields, stone walls and particularly fine breeds of creamy lambs. The only lambs here were at the local slaughterhouse from whence came piteous cries and the inns where stew bubbled all day long on greasy stoves.

The unmarried women showed bare legs and breasts to the passing seamen and often had left their children alone in tiny airless backrooms, so George reported, scandalized.

Bess, Joyce's mother and Wilkie came to Newcastle for the first time when Joyce was big with her baby and only then because she pleaded with George to allow them there. He had refused to have any of her family anywhere near their home before this. Joyce knew that she would need help when the baby was born.

Her mother was ten minutes in the house before she started cleaning the kitchen. George shut himself up in what they called his study, a tiny room in the depths of the house where he wrote sermons few people ever came to the church to hear. There he consumed vast quantities of cooking sherry.

The church itself was damp and freezing even in August, surrounded as it was by the airless buildings of the docks and only a few faithful middle-aged women turned up for the services. No wonder, Joyce thought, he disliked it all so much.

Joyce's first baby was born and was a boy. She was glad of that, at least George should be proud to have a son. When he was allowed into the room he looked fondly at her for the first time since their hasty wedding.

'Well done, Joyce,' he said, lightly, 'he's a bonny boy.'

'He looks just like you, George,' Joyce responded loyally and won from him a smile.

The fact was, she thought, that George

liked being in bed with her. It was possibly the only part of being married which he did like. He didn't seem too keen on her cooking, she didn't blame him for that but she did blame him for the way he looked so carefully at the food she put on the table.

She wanted to say to him that he did not earn sufficient money to start being picky about his food but the thing was that she was a little afraid of him, not physically but of the things he said. George had what people called 'a way with words' and Joyce felt nervous speaking when he was there or when other people were there.

'I shall have to go to war in my official capacity if it comes to it,' he said to her during the early summer of that year.

'Go to war?' She had not thought of it. Her heart could not help lightening at the idea of not being with George, of the possibility of not having to stay here by herself.

'Why yes, what did you think I would do?'

'I don't know.'

'You can go back to Heath Houses,' George said, 'I'm sure your father and mother will be glad of your company and you'll be safer there.'

Joyce was almost happy at the idea. If George could go off to what he called 'ministering to the spiritual need of the soldiers' then she could certainly go back to Heath

Houses with Matthew, her baby. She wrote to her mother to ask if it would be all right and had the reply that the door was always open, they would be pleased to see her.

It was one of the best days she had had since she had left the nursing school in tears when Joyce returned to Durham with Matthew. At first there seemed little to do but she said to her mother shortly after getting there,

'If you would see to Matthew, if it wouldn't be too much trouble I could volunteer to work at one of the local hospitals. Matthew's an easy baby, he's sleeping all night now. I know I'm not properly qualified but I did most of the work and they need people to aid the nurses. The pay probably isn't much–'

Her mother stopped her there.

'I think it's a very good idea,' Bess said.

Nine

By the time war was declared in September of 1939, Iris and Wilkie had been nursing at Darlington for several months. David had finished university and joined his father in the business.

He loved ships and shipping and would have wanted to go into the navy except that his father expected him to carry on the foundry.

It would have been foolish not to and his father also had had one or two bad turns lately, nothing important, just tiredness, going home early, falling asleep but then he had had the responsibility of the business by himself for so long. Such things took their toll of men and he was proud that David was there, Iris knew in the way that he spoke about his son to other people when she was present.

She went out on to the terrace at home in the early evening, desperate to tell some-body the decision she had not voiced and joined David, saying abruptly, 'Wilkie and I are going to see if we can go and nurse abroad.'

He turned, having not heard her, she

thought. He was about to speak but she had forestalled him, sensing that he would be left at home and that it was the very last place he wanted to be.

He sighed and looked out across the garden, past the lawns, the trees at the bottom, the way that the open space came so quickly at the end of the houses.

'It's so dull,' he said.

'Better dull than dead.'

He looked at her then.

'Have you told the parents yet that you're going?'

'No,' she admitted.

'Hadn't you better?'

'I don't know if I'll be accepted.'

'Are they in a position to turn down even you?'

'What a very brotherly thing to say,' she said and they both smiled.

She and Wilkie had to go to London to see whether they would be accepted to be Queen Alexandra nurses. There was a medical to get through and then a selection board at the War Office in Whitehall. Iris didn't see why they shouldn't be accepted but it was hard going, sitting in front of people, having questions shot at you and they so much older than you, so much more knowledgeable.

She did the best she could. She knew they were short of nurses but she and Wilkie had only just become qualified. Would it stand in her way? She didn't think it would.

Somehow the tone of the whole thing was reassuring and unlike Wilkie, who went in there nervous, believing that she would not end up going, Iris knew from the very beginning that she would. She could hardly believe in her own confidence but was glad of it, answered the questions and kept her chin up and in the end they were both told that they would be accepted.

'I never wanted to stay here and nurse, I really didn't,' she said as they enthused. 'I thought they might keep us here.'

'The vast unknown. How will I tell my mam and dad? I didn't think we'd find out so soon, I thought it would be weeks before we knew.'

'You didn't tell them you were coming?' Iris said.

'I didn't like to, especially with Joyce being stuck as she is.'

'They must be very keen to have us.'

'Are you frightened?'

'Not a bit,' Iris assured her but she was.

Wilkie didn't know how to tell her parents that she would very likely be sent overseas. In the end she didn't have to. She fell over the words as she sat in the shabby little front room with her parents. Her mam said to her, 'We know you have to do your bit and we don't want you worrying on about us. We did hope you might stay here–'

'I might yet–'

'They're going to need nurses in France almost straight away,' her dad said. Her dad, having nothing much better to do, was always ahead with the news as he read his *Evening Chronicle* from cover to cover. 'You'll come back speaking like the Frogs and wanting their legs for tea.'

Her dad made fun of things when he was upset and she thought she was lucky to have him for a dad. He was good to them and you couldn't say that of everybody's dad. She went over and kissed him and then, for good measure, she kissed her mam too and nobody said they might miss her.

It was worse when she told Joyce.

'It won't all be plain sailing, you know,' Wilkie said when they were standing together in the back street, the only privacy they could have.

Joyce looked squarely at her for the first time.

'I'll look after Mam and Dad,' she said and then she added quickly, 'You will take care of yourself, won't you?'

Wilkie hugged her and assured her and then she was gone and Wilkie wished for the fiftieth time that Joyce had been going with them.

As she put down her bags Iris heard the door of the sitting room open and her mother, seeing her in the heat of the hall stopped for a moment, said, 'Oh my dear, come in,' and came towards her, enfolding her into an embrace and Iris knew that she did not have to explain anything.

When they let go of one another her mother turned away, saying briskly, 'Your father and David aren't back yet. Shall we sit in the garden?'

Home, Iris discovered as they sat, drinking coffee, was never so dear as when you were leaving. How many times had she wanted to get away? Now she would have given almost anything not to go, she was sick with nerves at the idea.

At teatime when the men returned from the office at the end of the day they hugged her. They too knew what it meant. She couldn't look at either of her parents, somehow it was her father who made her feel emotional and she had a hard time telling him that she had been accepted to be a Queen Alexandra nurse. There was silence for a few moments and then he said softly,

'I thought you would but nothing was certain before now. There was a very selfish part of me which didn't want you to go but I knew you would and I knew they would want you.'

'Did you?' She very much needed him to

139

be proud of her.

'Certainly, being the lass you are. I knew you wouldn't marry Johnny Fenwick and have children and be content with that. It wasn't right for you.'

'I may live to regret it.'

'Possibly, but people can only do what seems right for them at the time.'

Her mother said nothing much more. Iris went to her. She knew the way her mother had one hand up to her lips that she was crying.

'Mother–'

'I know.' Her mother's voice was trembling but yet contained as she always was. Iris loved her so much for her control when she would rather her daughter stayed here where at least for the moment it was safe. 'I know but I'm so afraid ... that I'm going to lose you.'

Iris tried to be reassuring. It was strange; she had not thought until now that she might die. When it was very late and the sun had sunk down beyond the houses, she and David sat in the living room.

'I wish I could go,' he said.

'You can't leave Daddy. Besides, you're doing vital war work. Where would we be without our ships?'

'Yes, but whatever would I do if anything happened to you? You've always been there and I never had any desire to be an only child.' He spoke lightly and in one way Iris knew that he did not want to speak of the awful possibilities of war but since she was going it was important to tell her now how much she meant to him.

'Another gin and tonic would be a life saver,' she said, smiling, and David replenished their glasses and the few moments gave them time for the silence to absorb the words.

On the morning she left, with her trunk packed, he came to her in her room and there they said goodbye and Iris's throat hurt for how she had not cried.

As they embraced she said, 'You will look after Daddy and Mother, won't you?'

'I'll do my best. You will be careful?'

And then he was gone.

Ten

It was easier after Iris left Durham, though being considered a part of the army was not something she had imagined. Iris thought she would never get used to saluting, to calling other people by their second names. It was October 1939 and already a few nurses were in France and hundreds more were now set to follow.

Cherbourg was the first place Iris reached that autumn in France. They had come by ship, nothing but a mattress to sleep on, the portholes blacked and everything shadowed and quiet, but inside they sang the songs of the day and danced. A British destroyer kept them company at first and then a French destroyer.

She had gone to Southampton by train, excited, glad that she and Wilkie were being kept together, she didn't think she could have faced it without her friend. She even thought she had said so blatantly when they were interviewed and Wilkie had said the same. Things were so much easier when there were two of you. Wilkie reported that her parents had reacted just as Iris's had, hard as it was for them.

'My dad is so poorly and Mam has to run the shop by herself and I don't like to leave them.'

'They'll have your pay.'

'I have promised them every penny I make.'

'Of course you have,' Iris said, carefully not looking at her in case Wilkie was crying which she didn't do much of, in fact Iris couldn't remember Wilkie crying, even when Joyce had had to marry George.

Iris found a friendly face from home, Tom Cruickshank. He had used to come to the dances when they were all eighteen, which was beginning to be such a long time ago. The soldiers spent most of their time digging trenches and Tom was enthusiastic, organized, kind.

To her surprise there was very little to do and soldiers with nothing to distract them either imagined they were ill or found small troubles which became bigger troubles when they had nothing more to think about, so it was exasperating in a way for the nurses.

Iris could not decide what was worse, the fact that there were no casualties or the relief that so few men were being hurt or killed. She had to remind herself that there was always a lot of waiting during a war but it was so difficult to do nothing.

As the weather became colder the usual winter illnesses were brought in, chest infections were the main problem. Very cold weather brought pneumonia and bronchitis. The sleet and rain and wind turned the area into a sea of mud and it was impossible to keep one's uniform looking anything like as clean as she wanted it to be.

Iris regarded the snow outside the tents with dismay. She had always thought of France as somewhere sunny with good food, like holidays, not as inches of snow and she had not nursed in difficult conditions like these before. It was cold everywhere except near the stoves. She thought of what it would be like at home, sitting over a big fire, sleeping in a soft bed, safe inside with the bitter weather beyond the thick stone walls of her home.

To be so cold all of the time seemed to make everybody miserable. At Christmas she was more homesick than she had ever been in her life. All she could think about was the possibility of the spring, of warmer weather, but at least with nothing for the soldiers to do there were invitations from both British and French units to parties and Iris danced with lots of men and learned to drink Cointreau.

The first sight of spring flowers brought with it an advancement of the war and there was very soon enough work even for Iris to forget all about her home. Denmark was invaded in April, the Low Countries in May.

The war, as far as she was concerned, had really begun. It was thought that they were ready to fight but ideas of fighting were different. The British had been ready to fight the Great War again and their ideas were the same but Hitler had different methods, mostly from the air. The Allied soldiers were taken by surprise.

British and French went forward as the Germans advanced and refugees poured into France with whatever they could carry. Iris saw many of them and could not help being glad and selfish that her family were, for the moment at least, safe in Durham.

The German planes bombed the roads and civilian casualties were many, old and young. Doctors and nurses working at the front were sending soldiers to the hospitals and ambulance trains brought the wounded in but even the red cross showing so blatantly on them did not stop the Luftwaffe from attacking them, maybe she thought, they just couldn't see them properly for the dust, at least it brought her comfort to think so. Who would deliberately do such things?

The Allies were now in a line across the country but the Germans broke through and rumours of what was happening was so frightening that nobody wanted to hear the gossip, most of which, Iris thought, could not be true. She was afraid for the first time that the Germans might invade England, that the war would be lost here, that there was nothing to be gained, that the Allies' line would not hold.

The air attacks increased and the base hospital where Iris and Wilkie stayed was bombed. It was the most horrible thing that had ever happened but she was not frightened, she had not time to be. Casualties came in from the trains and she must reassure her patients and shield those who could not be moved as the night went on, from the noise and the fear.

Within a week the German armoured divisions crashed through the French army and began to make their way to the Channel ports and the whole Allied armies with their medical units began retreating towards the sea and the Channel ports. It grieved her that patients were moved before they were well enough to go. It was frightening to be working as the sound of gunfire drew closer and closer until there was no more time to stay and the nurses were taken in ambulances before the Germans drew any nearer.

Iris had never thought of herself as a brave person but she would have been inclined to argue, had it been considered acceptable. She did not want to go and leave her patients behind and the others felt the same.

Retreat was horrible, she decided. Absconding in the moonlight, like they were doing a flit, the German army moving closer all the time. In the darkness hundreds of refugees moving towards the coast and every time they came within distance of it they were turned back as the German troops shelled the area.

It was strange but she was not afraid. She did begin to think though that she might not make it home. Ships were being shelled in the harbours, ambulance trains full of casualties were attacked, was the word. Villages they went through were aflame in the night.

They ended up walking, like many other people, after the ambulance broke down and could not be started and although other vehicles passed them they were all overloaded with wounded soldiers. The towns they passed through could be seen through the glow of fire, ruined farmhouses all along the roadside. Iris and Wilkie eventually arrived, hungry, thirsty, filthy, more tired than she could remember having been before, at Cherbourg. Iris could have cried.

A British ship lay there as though waiting for her. She felt guilty that other people were not allowed on board. Iris long remembered the empty towns destroyed, the looting, the hopeless faces of the refugees, how guilty she felt at being on a ship bound for England, knowing that other ships had been blown up and she might not make it back. Some were destroyed even before they left the harbour.

Was England to be next? It made her sick to think about it.

King's Cross looked so normal. How had she expected it to look? Teatime in summer. People going home from their work in the city.

Standing on the station and all around people in uniform, lots of them and an atmosphere about the place such as she had never seen before. She had a terrible desire to burst into tears and had to suppress it. Nobody else was doing such ridiculous things. It was only then that she noticed the blood on her clothes, the grime on her hands and the way that she would have given almost anything she owned for a cup of tea.

Her legs were like lead but there seemed nowhere to sit down and she wished for maybe the fiftieth time that she was not alone and for the hundredth time that she was at home, and she thought, lots of people, thousands maybe over the years have stood here in this station and known it was the last step before home, the sound of British accents thick.

She wished and wished there was a train right now. Her legs ached. She began to envision the journey north, the rush through Stevenage, the passing of Peterborough, the feeling that you were almost home when you reached Doncaster. She loved trains, the way the rain hit the windows and how if you craned your neck at one particular point nearer home you could see the white horse marked out in chalk upon the hillside.

She loved the little fields, the neat hedge-rows, the sun setting low on the horizon, the plain of York where there was nothing to stop the wind across the ploughed fields, and best of all the dark outlines of the castle and the cathedral when you reached Durham, when you finally got home.

The tears were running down her cheeks, much to her surprise. She wiped them away, head down so that nobody should notice. People had gone through terrible times, she must not cry. She was on the way home, she would be back later that day.

It was only when her legs ached so much from standing that she could hardly bear them any more that the train was finally there and she hurried up the platform towards it and there was something about the man hurrying two people in front that she thought she recognized.

Her heart beat hard and fast and her tongue turned to jelly but she managed somehow to get ahead and catch him up. As she reached his sleeve he paused and stopped, ready with a rough word she could see because he too was tired to exhaustion but his mouth stayed itself when he saw who she was. His face was lined and covered in dirt. It was Johnny. She called his name twice before he heard her, before he stopped and turned and she saw the joy amidst the tiredness.

His face lit up and there on the platform, oblivious to the people hurrying past, he took her into his arms just as though nothing had gone wrong and he said, 'Oh, Iris, how completely wonderful you are.'

It made her laugh and then she could feel the tears of release running down her cheeks, such as she had not allowed them to until now. She was in his arms, perhaps it was the only place left of any safety.

All the horrors eased and went away and were replaced by the feelings of love which she would always have for him and then the dismay, that she should have married him, that she had let him go, how could she have known, how could she have done such a stupid thing and then she was angry for the choices that women must make. Would he have loved her had she been the agreeable person that would have married him? Did he love his wife for those qualities?

He kissed her. Iris thought that it was without question the most wonderful kiss in the whole history of the entire universe and she heard the sweet sound of Geordie voices around her, though the men were tired and beaten, urging him on to kiss her again.

She laughed and for just a few seconds

everything was as it should be and she was more and more aware of how for many hundreds of people nothing would ever be as it should again. The world was a different place for all of them now.

'Do your family know you're coming home?'

'Nobody knows. I haven't had a chance to do anything other than travel.' She was beginning to feel as though she would never get home, she had been travelling for so many days and seen so many tired faces, homeless people, injured children, endured so much for so long she scarcely knew what month it was, never mind what day.

'Is there some way you could let them know you're safe but won't be back yet?'

Iris eased herself from him. 'Why?' She had wanted to go home so much. She looked into his eyes, not understanding, and then finally grasped his intent and was amazed. 'You mean—'

'I do.'

'What about Nan?'

'I telephoned my father and he's with her and they know I'm safe but I only said that I would be back as soon as I could. What if we just had tonight?'

Every decent instinct told Iris she ought to refuse, that she should have insisted he go back to Durham but then she could not insist, she could just go back herself and even though she knew they cared about her they would not understand. Nobody except the people who had been in France would understand the enormity of what had happened.

'Twenty-four hours,' he said, 'that's all.'

'Where would we go?'

'Come on, or there'll be no seats left,' he said and he was right, it was packed. He managed to get her a seat, the men gave theirs up when they saw, she thought, the blood and grime on her uniform. He sat down on the floor with his back against the seat and gazed up at her and she thought he had the most beautiful eyes that she had ever seen.

Even in such circumstances she had to stop herself from asking stupid questions about his home and his wife as though to reassure themselves that nothing had changed.

He bought her tea and biscuits. Never had anything tasted so good. Iris had had nothing to eat or drink that day and she could not remember the last time she had eaten something she enjoyed. It was strange how normal the train seemed, people going home and many of them asked questions, wanted to know what had happened.

She did not want to talk about it and kept staring out of the window and left Johnny to discuss the war, she was so tired and now that she was here none of it seemed real, yet she thought she would always see before her the people who had nowhere to go, the little towns being destroyed, the threat of the German soldiers ever advancing, the way that the noise of the bombing didn't stop. Even now it went on and on in her head and it was so frightening.

It looked as though they could not be stopped. They seemed invincible. She remembered the retreating troops. Strangely it was not shameful, it was the best thing to do but if the war was to go on like this what hope was there? If nobody could stop them whatever would happen? What when they were marching on London?

She could not bear to think any more. She was here and the train was taking her back to her beloved north and that would have to be enough. Every moment was taking her away from the war and she would rest until she knew what to do next. Maybe she would never go back to nursing, she didn't know whether she could face any more.

At York, Johnny touched her arm and they got off and not far away, just as far as their tired bodies would carry them, they found a hotel. It was a wonderful hotel, Iris thought, it was possibly the most wonderful hotel in the entire history of the world. It was old-fashioned, had been a Victorian house. You went through a little archway to the gardens, the proprietor told them.

Eager for news he asked them about their ordeal and then showed them to an enormous room with a huge marble fireplace, a great big bed and a balcony which looked out into the darkness of the midsummer evening. They threw open the floor-to-ceiling windows and there in the moonlight they stood together and she could smell the flowers and it was so English somehow that she could not bear it.

'Don't cry,' he said to her hair.

'Whatever will we do now that the Germans have taken France?'

'We'll do whatever we have to.'

'The French must have said that to themselves.'

'The French didn't have the Channel. Thank God we have it.'

'But Hitler has–'

Johnny kissed her.

'It will never happen, not while there is a single British person to stop them. Don't fret. Forget about it now. Just for tonight. Let's have tonight. It may be the only time we can spend together. We have to go back to our lives but not now.'

They went downstairs, having tidied themselves as best they could considering neither had any luggage, and the couple who owned the hotel had found them a decent bottle of claret. Iris thought she had not tasted anything as good in years. There were eggs, vegetables fresh from the garden and some kind of pudding like carrot cake. It reminded Iris of Scotland and having carrot cake in the Highlands when she was on holiday there with her parents as a little girl.

They had brandy to take to bed and there in the big quiet bedroom with nothing but a candle or two she kissed him as she had wanted to kiss him since they had stopped seeing one another. They didn't sleep, it would have been such a waste of time. They did not speak of Nan or her family or Durham at first and she told him that she loved him, that she had never loved anyone as she loved him.

He laughed and he said, 'Why on earth wouldn't you marry me?'

'What, and miss all this?'

He didn't say anything and Iris was inclined to cry for some ridiculous reason but all she could think to say was,

'Don't you love Nan?'

'Yes, of course.' His voice was unsteady.

'I would have made you a dreadful wife.'

'The worst.'

'You would have hated me.'

'I do hate you.' Iris waited for a few moments and then he looked at her. 'I'm so glad we had this, it's the only good thing about the war, it urges people to do splendidly stupid things as they never would in peacetime. I thought I could have every-thing.'

'Haven't you had everything?'

'I have now,' he said, and kissed her.

Finally in the dawn, exhausted, they slept.

She awoke thinking she was still in France with her patients and must get up and attend to them and it was such a delight to find herself close in his arms and the sunlight edging around the curtains. She shut her eyes and remembered that she was back in England away from the war. She was sorry for all those people who were still there and for those who had terrible problems but she could not help being so pleased she was here.

They spent the day in bed but by evening could not put off any longer. They had to go home. They washed and dressed, thanked their host and caught the next train back to Durham.

There could be no private conversation but anyway what more would she and Johnny have said? In normal times he could have berated her for what she had done, told her how much better off he was now with his wife, how much he loved her, and she could have told him that she regretted nothing or everything and they could have done that safe in the knowledge that nothing else mat-tered, but it was not so any more. Nobody wanted to talk.

She was only glad to be going north and with the sound of the train and the raindrops trickling down the window she thought with every heartbeat that she was going back to Durham and he was safe and that was all that was important any more.

When the train finally stopped he had fallen asleep.

'Johnny,' she murmured, and when he didn't respond, 'Johnny, we're almost home.'

They were, she thought, the best words in the language. He stirred, looked about him and then up at her smiling wearily.

The train finally halted. They got off, craning their necks for sight of the cathedral and castle, the winding River Wear, but it was dark by then and all they could catch were shadows and together they went to a telephone kiosk on the station. David answered when she rang.

'David, it's me.'

'Oh, thank God. Where are you?'

'The station.'

'Our station?'

'What other station is there?' she said, almost happy.

'I'll be there in five minutes.'

Iris went outside, and watched Johnny as he telephoned.

'My father's coming for me,' he said as he stepped outside.

'David is for me.'

'Why don't we walk down the hill?'

The road twisted first one way and then the other. She saw David's car before they reached the bottom and stopped.

'Goodbye, then, Johnny.'

'Goodbye, old girl,' he said as though they were just friends and then made nonsense of it by taking her into his arms. She was glad of the darkness, glad to give in to that kiss and when she could sustain it no longer for respectability's sake and the fact that David had halted the car and was waiting for her across the way, she let go of him. David was out of the car.

'Does he want a lift, the soldier?'

'No, somebody's coming for him.'

'Where's your luggage?'

'In France.' Her voice wobbled. David hugged her.

'Don't worry,' he said, 'soon have you home.'

She got in, David started up the car, they drove very carefully considering the restrictions.

'Anybody special?'

'What?'

'The man you were kissing?'

'No.'

David was, she thought, too sensitive to ask any more. They reached home. Her parents were hovering in the hall, gathered her to them as she stepped into the house. Her mother's voice was broken when she tried to speak, her father's was almost there too.

'We thought...' her mother said, and then more practically, 'Are you hungry? You must be. Come in, come in.'

They seated her in a big chair. More tea, toast, cake. Nothing had ever tasted quite so welcome, so wonderful. Although she could sense they wanted to ask her a great many questions they did not, fearing or perhaps knowing that to have to go through any of the situation again would be too much for her self-control.

She had a bath which was bliss, her mother found her a nightdress. Later, however, when the house was quiet and she thought everybody had gone to bed she heard the door and David whispered, 'May I come in?'

'Yes, do.'

David came in, sat down on the bed, juggling a brandy decanter and two glasses and regarded her with affection.

'Just like when we were younger,' she said.

'Except the brandy,' said David, pouring generously and handing her a big balloon glass. 'I'm so glad to see you, so pleased. We've all been so very worried about you.'

'It's already more than I could ever have hoped for,' she said, sipping and then closing her eyes, the further to enjoy the taste of the alcohol. It reminded her of the night before and she was glad then that she and

Johnny had had that one night together. Brandy would always remind her of him and it was lovely to be back with her parents and David, it made her never want to leave again.

'It was Johnny, wasn't it?' David guessed.

She opened her eyes.

'I met him by chance at King's Cross. He looked awful, so tired, so beaten.'

'He's not and neither are we.'

Iris nodded and sipped at her brandy.

'Are you all right?' David asked.

'I feel so lucky. There were so many people desperate to get on a ship and they let us through, the nurses. I'll never forget the faces of those people who were left and the ... the refugees by the roadside in France, homeless and hurt and...'

They had some more brandy, Iris had thought she would not sleep, that her dreams would be haunted by blood, injury, death and the almost overwhelming desire for being at home and not able to attain it but there was no such problem.

When David had gone the room was full of thick comforting darkness like oversized cushions and she could hear, beyond the window, the sound of rain like music, gentle against the glass. She was safe now, nothing could hurt her here.

Jack Fenwick got out of the car and

embraced his son.

'We thought you might have made it back yesterday,' he said.

'I thought so too.' Damn it, did his father always know everything? 'It's been so difficult.'

'Of course. Nan is keen to see you and the boys are excited.'

'It was good of you to come for me.'

'Nonsense. I was here anyway.'

'I thought you'd be in London.'

'I came back here to be with Nan when we heard how badly things were going and... I had to go to the works.'

'Thanks, I appreciate it. I know how busy you are.'

'We were so worried. When you rang from London I thought you'd be home sooner.'

'Yes, I expected to. You know what the trains are like.'

His father said nothing and the silence grew until Johnny felt obliged to fill the gap.

'Dad–'

'It's all right, whatever it is.'

'Please, stop a minute.'

They were down the hill and into the town by then but Jack obligingly pulled the car over in the middle of the market place, which was empty of cars, there being no petrol for people unlike him, who needed to move around so much. There were people about and it was a beautiful summer's evening, mild and with a full moon. He sat there and finally his father broke the quietness by saying softly,

'I don't know what hell war is, I've never been that far. I would say let's go and have a drink but Nan is expecting us any minute, it wouldn't be fair to her–'

'No, I know. I ... I know. I just...'

'The boys are wonderful.'

Johnny stared out of the window at his side, unable to see anything, his emotions having finally bettered him.

'I wanted to come home so much, so very much but I ... I feel grubby now. I let her down, you see.'

He heard the smile in Jack's voice.

'Oh, lad,' he said, 'don't be so hard on yourself. All that matters is that you came back.'

'I didn't want to. I wanted to – to run off. Did you ever?'

'Did I ever what?'

'Were you ever unfaithful to my mother?'

Jack did laugh but shortly.

'You always tell me how much you adored her,' Johnny said, 'like it was a pure–'

'There was nothing pure about it,' Jack said in a hard voice, 'we were just people and we made stupid mistakes.'

Johnny let go of his breath and then said, 'I spent the night in York with Iris Black.'

Several seconds went by. Johnny counted

them before his father said, 'Iris was very special to you. Is she all right?'

'She's gone home to her family now.'

'Good. Are you ready to go back to yours?'

Johnny nodded and his father started up the car and for the first time then Johnny was glad to be back in Durham.

Jack felt his son hesitate when he got out of the car but the boys had seen him. Nan let them out of the house and they ran across the gravelled drive toward their father. Johnny moved forward eagerly then and Jack thought with relief that however much his son wanted Iris Black she could never be like this for him.

The two little boys shouted, 'Daddy! Daddy!' and flung themselves at whichever bit of Johnny they could reach.

Eleven

The most awful thing about being at home was that Iris didn't know what to do. At first all she wanted was never to leave again and she knew that she was due leave but after nothing more than a few days she began to feel left out. How stupid.

She went to Heath Houses. She and Wilkie had been parted when they got back to England, so she had known that Wilkie was safe and would be making her way back to Durham but had not seen her and they ended up embracing in tears in the back lane behind Wilkie's parents' little house.

'How are you?'

'Bored,' Wilkie said, crying and laughing.

'Me too,' Iris said, doing the same. 'Aren't we stupid?'

'We have to get back or at least we have to go on. What else is there for us?'

'I was going to say that nothing could be worse than France but I won't because you never know.'

'We couldn't do another retreat like that, we just couldn't,' Wilkie said and they stood back and looked at each other.

'It's funny, for some reason it didn't feel

altogether like a retreat in some ways,' and then she thought she would never forget the faces on the soldiers, all that work, all that effort and they hadn't got it right and their commanders hadn't got it right. They were trying to fight the Great War for the second time and the Germans were too clever for them. They must think of something else, of something new, and they must fight again.

'I just wish Joyce was coming with us next time,' Wilkie said, 'but she's doing such good work here.'

Iris's mother didn't even cry when she left but she whispered at the railway station, where Wilkie's parents saw them off too, having been collected by car by David,

'I'm so proud of my only daughter. Go on, darling, do your bit.'

'I'll try.'

She couldn't speak to her father, she just embraced him. David nodded at her and Wilkie's parents had to be hugged too and then they were away and even though she watched until everybody was out of sight and she was sorry, she could not help the little frisson of excitement. This was what she was meant to be doing. She was not supposed to be sitting at home. This was right, nothing had ever felt like it.

It was midnight when they left England. There had been fog earlier but as they pulled away from the docks the fog went, the moon came out and the ship began to move. Up on deck Iris and Wilkie could see that there were lots of little boats in the bay with tiny lights at both ends and the naval escort with them, moving out.

The tiny cabin they had been allotted had been fitted out with six bunks when it was really big enough for four and the only other thing in the room was a cupboard for their belongings and a sink for washing. Iris could not imagine how they would manage there for a few days, never mind however long it would take them to get to their destination. They were not allowed to open the portholes and everything was in darkness at night and they must not throw anything overboard in case it betrayed their whereabouts to the enemy.

They could wear their pyjamas at night but must wear clothes on top. It was very uncomfortable but the presence of the other nurses in their cabin was a great help since they were all literally in the same boat. Nobody cried, at least not so as you could hear even in the quietness of the night, and they spent time talking, learning one another's history, playing games and drinking tea.

In the mornings they could go on deck. There were a great many men to very few women and even Wilkie had interested men around her, something she said privately that she had never experienced before and intended to enjoy.

Iris was still thinking of Johnny and the night they had spent together and though she kept telling herself that she should fall in love with someone else there was no way you could do such a thing, and the more she tried the less it worked.

She was happy to dance when there was the opportunity but she did not want to go outside and kiss anybody in the moonlight. Some men were perceptive and did not trouble her, others were happy to dance.

Those who persisted she froze out and many was the night she ended up in the cabin by herself while the others made the best of their time on board, knowing there would be a great deal of work to do whenever they got to where they were going. It was beginning to feel endless.

There was however one bright spark: Tom Cruickshank, whom she had known all her life, was there. He seemed to turn up when he was needed and she was glad of him. His father was some kind of professor at the university. His mother was one of her mother's friends and she and Tom had been small children together, being the same age and being taken to playgrounds together from when they could walk, and he had been one of her first partners at dances as they grew older.

Tom soon understood the situation and kept a watchful eye and if any man became too amorous he would come along and rescue her. She felt safe with him, it was rather as though David was there, he was a piece of home. They would talk about their parents, their friends and he knew that she had turned down Johnny Fenwick and that Johnny had since married but he was far too sensitive to refer to it.

They sailed east and it began to get very much warmer. At night they would stay on deck in an attempt to catch at any breeze. Some of the best times of the voyage were standing outside with Tom, talking about home.

Iris helped in the sick bay when there was anything to do, just for the change, but the men on board were well and fit and she must be glad of that, instead of wishing for something more to do.

Finally then, the Middle East. The fighting was in Sudan, Palestine and where they finally stopped, Egypt, none of them places Wilkie or Iris had imagined going and so far from home that she dreamed of being back in her bed in Durham within the sound of the cathedral bells.

General Wavell forced the Italians from Cyrenaica and was then obliged to turn his attention to Greece so North Africa suffered from lack of troops. The Germans were threatening to overrun the Allied armies. There was now a possibility, which nobody voiced, that the Germans would win so much that the war would be lost.

What was left of the depleted Eighth Army after so many men went off to Greece retreated from the frontier a hundred miles to El Alamein where there is no more than forty miles between the sea and the salty marsh of the Qattara Depression. The commander, General Auchinleck, had replaced Wavell after the final evacuation of Greece and tried to recapture Cyrenaica. And when pushed back in early 1942 decided that he would retreat no further.

In the north the road and railways were over desert at not much distance from the salt lagoons which fringed the sea. In the middle were hills and, beneath nothing more than a covering of sand, was rock.

To the south the rock is much more visible and finally becomes a sheer cliff to the Qattara Depression. The Nile Valley was like a fortress. Only an attack from the front would do. This General Rommel tried to do.

General Alexander would not give in. He had been at Dunkirk; he would not have this be another Dunkirk. His men would stand and die if necessary but they would not retreat, they would not give in. General Montgomery took over the Eighth Army.

The Germans called the Allies 'rats' and the soldiers there became proud to be the desert rats.

The Germans broke through but the Eighth Army hit back for three days. After that there was a six-week period during which nothing happened and General Alexander used this time for training and it was then that extra supplies arrived in Egypt. Between the German defeat in September and the battle the following month the Allied air forces destroyed essential supplies and British submarines dealt with tankers. Many ships were sunk and the supplies lost and the Allies were not often attacked from the air because the enemy aircraft were either on the ground because there was no fuel or had been destroyed.

The Battle of Egypt began on Friday October 23, 1942 in brilliant moonlight.

Huge areas had been mined, with machine guns between then. The mines had to be cleared before the infantry could advance and there had to be enough space to get the tanks through.

In all this the nurses worked. They had firstly to clean up the filthy hospital buildings and lived inside the hospital as it was the only place fit for habitation.

Casualties soon began to arrive by ambulance from where doctors worked in the field and trains also brought the injured soldiers to the base hospitals. The theatres were working all the time and hundreds of casualties came in. At first a man's fate in the hospitals was decided by his seniority or rank but this was pushed aside by the doctors and nurses. They could not accept this kind of military rule and very soon it was the worst cases which were seen first, no matter who they were.

On night duty Iris went around the huts with a little hurricane lamp, on the very edge of the desert, hearing the jackals calling. She thought there could not have been any more torments than there were.

Water became very scarce and was rationed and it was brown and looked most unappetizing. The views were of nothing but sand and she longed for England, for even the sight of grass. There were huge swarms of flies so that the men's wounds moved with maggots and were cleansed. The dust got in everywhere. The fleas in the beds were a constant torment. The rats were enormous and ran over you when you slept. There was not sufficient water for washing nor for washing clothes and the work went on until she could not see for tiredness.

Casualties were more and more until there were no more beds and there was not enough of anything. They went on doing the work they could, tirelessly. Iris forgot that there was any other kind of life but this. The only relief was sleep and there she could not worry about the way that the war was going or the idea that there would be Germans in London.

She tried to worry about what would happen when England was invaded and about her family, whether they would end up homeless or worse, whether the foundry would be bombed. She was glad of the work to distract her, she had never worked so hard nor expected to.

She fell asleep on her little bunk every night and did not care for the conditions or the hardships, all she must do was to try to ease the pain of sick and dying men and be glad of their gratitude, their fortitude. She did not understand how they could fight under such conditions. What kind of bravery did such things?

One night – she didn't even know what day it was, she scarcely knew what month or season it was just that the heat was unbearable and yet they bore it and they bore the flies on their food and the ants in the men's beds and the fleas in their own and the lack of washing – she gradually became aware of Wilkie standing over her as she dressed a leg wound. She could only just see her from the corner of her eye.

'What is it?' Iris said impatiently.

Wilkie hesitated over her.

'Spit it out. I haven't time for whatever

172

new problem somebody has devised.'

They were often hampered by government regulations and she was having none of it. Somehow Wilkie never had good news, it was always something fresh, always something dire. Iris was too busy, had been too busy for so many days now.

'Iris...' Wilkie stopped there.

Irritated, Iris finally stood up. Their makeshift hospital was almost falling down it had been bombed so hard. When the nurses had arrived there were no doors or windows and the sand storms were so bad and happened so often that they had placed blankets over all the gaps to keep out the sand and the dust. There were other problems, ants, stinking latrines, lack of beds, no clean linen, and scorpions. Iris tried not to think about the scorpions.

Her patient was sleeping now though how long he would survive in the state he was in she had no idea. She was beyond weary. She did not remember the last time she had stopped working except to sleep and then she would fall on her bed and be unconscious instantly.

There was never enough time to sleep until you began to dream on your feet of what it would be like to have enough rest to be refreshed. She had said so many comforting words to so many men that she could not think.

'What?' she said impatiently.

'They brought somebody in.'

'Somebody I know?'

Wilkie went on looking at her for a few moments before she said in quavering tones, 'Johnny.'

All Iris's worst dreams were caught up in this. She made her voice steady.

'Is he badly hurt?'

'Land mine in the abdomen.'

'Where is he?'

Wilkie took her to him.

The man lying on the bed did not look like the man she loved, he did not look like anybody and then he opened his eyes and was hers. He even smiled.

'Iris. What the hell are you doing here?'

She did not even have to attempt to keep her voice steady. It had been steady all those months in France and now here in Egypt. She had kept it steady while covering a patient with her body when they were being bombed, when so many young men all looking so like David had died, when they had lain and suffered rather than bother her, when jumped-up officers got in her way and tried to make her do things other than the way she had been taught and she had resisted and her voice had never quavered and she was not having it betray her because it was Johnny.

He was the man she loved. She had never

loved him more than she did now and it
would have been very cowardly indeed to let
him know how badly hurt he was. Her eyes
would not tell him so and neither would her
voice and she had done it so very many
times now and never owed it more to anyone than she did to Johnny.

'I could ask you the same question. Some
people will do anything to get out of it.'

'I can't feel anything.'

'Just as well,' Iris said, voice brisk. 'What
on earth were you doing?'

'Playing at soldiers,' he said.

She had to go, she had a lot of work to do
and just as well her horrid sensible self told
her and she must not think about him or she
would not be able to keep her mind on what
mattered.

'You'll be fine,' she said, 'I'll come back
later.'

There had been enough mistakes made in
this war, she thought, savagely, she must not
make more of them by negligence. She left
him to the care of the nurses who were on
his ward and went back to what she had
been doing and only her stubborn persis-
tence kept her there, dry-eyed throughout.

When she was finished, however, when she
was so tired that she could barely stand she
found herself going back to him, standing
over his bed and watching him even though
he was asleep. She was about to leave,

thinking she was seeing him for the last time, when he opened his eyes.

'Iris?' He caught at her hand. 'When you get back home don't let Nan know about us.'

She got down beside him and there she said gently, 'There's nothing to know.'

He looked at her and his eyes were vague but he said in broad Geordie, 'Aw, hinny, there's plenty to know,' and then in his own voice, 'I have loved you so very much all this time.'

'If it's any consolation I have wished a thousand times we had been married.'

'It's no bloody consolation at all,' he said, smiling a little.

'She made you a good wife, much better than I would ever have done.'

'You'd have been off with the first Tommy who looked twice at you.'

'I would. And you have your boys.'

'I know. I'm so pleased about that and they are wonderful.'

'Of course they are. Children always are.'

'Why aren't you looking after me?' he said.

'I am looking after you. What do you think I'm doing here?'

'You were right. This is what you were supposed to do. When you go home, you won't tell Nan.'

'You can tell her or not tell her as you choose.'

'Promise me. She's been good to me. I wouldn't have her hurt unnecessarily.'

'Don't think so little of me. I would never hurt anybody you loved.'

He looked narrowly at her because, she thought, he was in pain.

'I do love her.'

'It's all right. You don't have to ration the people you love. That would be stupid.' She smiled brilliantly at him.

'Oh, Iris,' he said and she thought how wonderful her name sounded on his lips. She remembered her name on his lips when they had drunk champagne in that stupid castle which his father owned and in the hotel in York and it was never better said than then. 'I think about the night we had after Dunkirk.'

'I think about that too. Go to sleep now and think about that. You're going to be all right. You aren't in pain?'

'No.' He, like so many other men, would not have told her even if he had been.

He closed his eyes and she kissed his forehead and then she would have lingered, she wanted to wait there but what kind of message would that convey? And yet he knew, she was aware of it, that he held her hand just a little longer and then he let go.

Johnny closed his eyes and thought of his beautiful wife and his children, his little boys and the far-off safety of Durham. His father would look after them, he knew. He was not going to make it back to England, he was not even going to make it through the night, he knew it. It didn't matter so very much, he had told Iris that he had had everything and it was true. There was nothing more to wish for.

The pain which he had denied had been bad to begin with and had been getting worse steadily. He was going into a sort of thick sweat and the thick sweat was getting in his eyes but when he tried to attract the attention of a nurse he did not seem to be able to get the words out.

The pain was creating a kind of screen between himself and the ward, and himself and the nurse and even himself and the bed somehow. The ward went into the distance whereas the pain grew nearer and harder to bear. There was nothing but the pain now.

He tried to distract himself again, thinking of Durham, but he did not know which was Durham and which was the pain. He had to concentrate very hard indeed against one and with the other and after a long time it felt stupidly and rather like when he had been a little boy and had an abscess in his ear and his mother had put a hot-water bottle on it. For hours and hours through the night and seemingly forever the pain went on but oh, the relief when the abscess finally burst and the pain stopped.

The darkness of the night had felt like it would not end but it did and all that was left was the heat of the hot-water bottle against his cheek. It felt like that now. After the pain had become unbearable the night went on and on and the dawn did not arrive and he wished and wished that it would, that the light would finally break. When he had lost hope, when he had lost sight of anything other than the blackness and the pain, the abscess burst. He was so glad, so filled with joy. It was over at last.

It seemed to him that it was like when he reached Durham after Dunkirk and Nan was giddy with pleasure and laughing. She was putting her arms around him and he felt safe there, like he had never felt before. She smelled of jasmine, that was what the smell was.

It was as if he had woken up from a dream and he had left behind the stink of war, the noise of battle, even the subdued sounds of the makeshift hospital. Iris was gone but somehow he did not mind, he was where he wanted to be, he was home.

Iris went off to bed and even as things were she did not stay awake, worrying, dreaming, thinking of what might happen, and the following day she had to get on, there were lots of other patients to consider. She could not leave them, there were so many and they all needed her.

Wilkie was looking after him. Iris wanted to go to him but she hadn't time. She hadn't even the time to ask about him. She didn't see Wilkie until they went off duty the following day and it was many hours later because of the incoming wounded.

'How's Johnny?' she said as they reached their quarters. Wilkie stood there like a big piece of stone and fussed, trying to get out of her uniform.

'He died,' she finally said when she was turned away. Her voice was harsh with tiredness and suppressed emotion and then it broke.

'I thought he would,' Iris said flatly because it was the only way she could get the words out. 'It wouldn't be much of a life with a colostomy bag and ... he wouldn't have survived much longer like that.'

'No,' Wilkie said. She didn't say it was for the best. Iris waited for the trite words, for any words because somehow any words were better than none, but Wilkie didn't say them because she couldn't, Iris could see.

Wilkie couldn't even look at her. They had both seen many men die before now but neither of them had had one die who mattered to them personally, though Iris regretted and was angry about each and every one and that included the enemy. They were just boys many of them, they hadn't lived yet and now...

They went to bed. The situation was so unreal that Iris persuaded herself it had not happened and was able to sleep, but every time she awoke, and it was many times, she knew that Johnny was dead and each time she was more aware of it. It was the greatest loss of her life. Nothing would ever equal it. That was her only comfort. Johnny Fenwick had been her best love and she would never forget him.

Twelve

Jack had not wanted to come up to the Newcastle works. He was tired but there was so much to be done always that he didn't sleep. As for eating he was never hungry any more and what he did eat was tasteless and when he did sleep his dreams were shot through with nightmares of endless pursuit from which he awoke covered in sweat.

His office desk was an ocean of papers so that he couldn't find anything, in spite of the fact that Mrs Gibson was always rearranging everything. She followed him about from London to Newcastle and back. Like most other people she had no home life, her husband, like thousands of others, was away fighting and the two of them had spent so much time in various hotels all over the place that he was certain people thought they were having some kind of raging affair.

They had even – God help us, he thought – slept in the same bed once or twice when the air raids were at their height, huddled together like children, hoping they weren't going to die but at least, as Tammy assured him, they wouldn't be alone when it happened, they would have somebody's arms around them and it was about as much as anybody could ask the way things were going.

'Tammy!' he roared. 'Where the bloody hell's the information on the...' and he stopped before the end of the sentence because she was already in front of him, slight, skinny, lips pursed up in disapproval at his impatience, a glint of anger in her eyes. They had long since cast aside any semblance of formality between them, except when other people were there but she said only, 'There's no need to shout.'

'I thought you were in the other room.'

She found what he was looking for without further ado and then she went back to get on with her typing and he found it soothing, listening to the click-clack of her fingertips upon the keys. She stopped.

There was a noise in the outer office and he looked up, he heard the door – the glass in it shuddered slightly when it was opened. He heard the murmur of soft voices. He didn't stop working. Whatever it was she could deal with it.

The voices went on long past the point where she should have got rid of whoever it was and he cursed inwardly as he did a hundred times a day at the interruption. The voices still went on and then there was silence. He listened for the shuddering of the glass as the intruder went out but nothing happened and after several seconds he was aware of Tammy standing in the doorway. He stopped writing and looked up.

'Whatever the hell is it now?' he said but he didn't go on.

He knew her too well. He had seen a similar look on her face in various offices, in the works, in hotel bedrooms, when there were air raids and she was trying to persuade him they should go to the nearest shelter and take cover and he was saying he had too much work to do to go anywhere, when there was a problem that would not be solved and they were both tired beyond bearing, and it was more than that.

Behind her stood another slight figure. He recognized her at once because she too had been with him through the hard times and he had tried to support her when Johnny went away, when the boys were born, when she had problems with them and with her life when Johnny was not there and when her mother was ill.

'Nan?' He got up from the desk and Tammy stood aside slightly but his daughter-in-law did not come forward so that he said, 'Nan?' again.

She was, he thought, the picture of grief. No charming boys tumbled about the office as they did occasionally when she knew he was in Newcastle and was tired of waiting for him to find enough time to come to her and she was determined that he should see them. He thought she stood there by will alone, nothing more was holding her up in the entrance to his office, where suddenly he was aware the day was grey with rain and it beat as it did in the town, dirty and dark upon the pavements and upon the windows. Nan had never been a large woman but now as he said, 'Nan, darling,' and she came forward into his arms he could feel the bones of her body, her wrists protruded through the sleeves of her coat as she put out her arms toward him, her face was tear stained but dry, her cheeks blanched.

'Oh, Jack, he's dead,' was all she managed.

Thirteen

It was November when the tide of battle turned and it was because of the work which Johnny and his men had done, clearing the ground of mines before the tanks could get through. The infantry prepared the ground for the tanks and the tanks waged another battle and they won through.

The first week of November was memorable for the enemy being chased out of Egypt, and the rain. Iris thought she would never forget the rain. At first it was welcome but it seemed after a day or two as if it would never stop. It took eight days to rid Egypt of the Germans and it was worth every second.

When things got easier Iris began to think about how Johnny might have survived and gone back to his wife and children. She felt so guilty about the night they had had together after Dunkirk. Maybe, she thought, I'm just naturally a wicked woman.

You did hear of such things though she had a suspicion that such phrases were coined by men. Was a wicked woman just somebody who was fighting for control of her own life? Was she the same kind of person as the prostitute who frequented Elvet Bridge at night who had a child at home?

Was she the woman who had been forced to choose when she wanted more than afternoon tea, babies' nappies and the drudgery of a house? God must be male, Iris decided, no female would ever have invented dust.

It had only been that one time with him, just that one time, she told herself, like somebody addicted. It was always just once more for the wicked woman, always just in case, while his wife probably sat dutifully at home, waiting for him. Maybe she didn't. Maybe she had found somebody else.

Iris didn't think so. She had the feeling that Nan adored him. The trouble was that now Nan would not have him either. She would never do stupid things with him like weeding the garden, going out for drinks with friends on Friday evenings, sitting by the fire on wintry Sunday afternoons.

I will never have any of that either, Iris thought wildly, because he is dead now. Those who are called upon to bear things do, that was the belief but Iris was just so glad they had had that night together after Dunkirk, it would live on in her memory as perfect. That shining day, the lovely little hotel, the clean sheets, the bottle of wine, the soft bed and she had told him that she loved him. If I never have anything like it ever again at least I will have had that, she thought.

The thoughts didn't last and now that the war in Egypt appeared to be over she wanted somebody to cling to and there were so many men, one of them had to be decent, one of them had to replace Johnny. Even her old dancing partner, Tom Cruickshank, had been killed but she was happy now to dance with anybody, to spend time with anybody, even to kiss anyone with willing lips.

Of the people left was Joe Coughtrey. It was enough that he came from Darlington. He had the right accent, she could talk to him of certain pubs and streets and he knew them. She arranged to meet him.

When she came off duty she was determined to glam herself up for him and went off and began to apply makeup in front of her tiny mirror. She heard a noise and when she turned around Wilkie was standing there in front of her.

With all the deprivations, Iris thought, Wilkie still managed her spectacular figure and Iris was impressed for the first time with the comfort of these things.

'I wish my mother was here,' she said. 'I miss her so much. I hope we get to go home soon.'

'So do I and I wish she was here too. She would talk some sense into you.'

'What do you mean?'

'You can't go on like this.'

'Oh, how wonderfully dramatic you are,'

Iris said, laughing.

'People will talk.'

'Now you're being funny.'

'No, it's important.' Wilkie took her arm as Iris tried to get past her. 'You can't go sleeping with half the army.'

'I haven't.'

'Not yet.'

'I don't know what you mean.'

'Yes, you do. You can't bring Johnny back and lying with your eyes closed in somebody else's arms sodden with gin isn't going to make it so. Your work here is more important than your personal grief. When we get out of here—'

'If.'

'When we get out of here you can cry your eyes out for eternity if you like but not now. The war is over here and we will go on and help and do other things and save other men and do better.'

'I loved him so much, Wilkie.'

'He was married to somebody else and had children. You could have married him but you chose not to. Don't go ruining your whole life over it,' Wilkie said.

There was a noise outside.

'That'll be Joe now,' Iris said, not moving.

Wilkie went over but Iris could hear her muffled tones as he said, 'Is Iris ready?'

'No, she isn't and she won't be. She's got more important things to do.'

Wilkie came back inside and closed the door.

Iris smiled through her tears.

'You can't talk to him like that, Wilkie, he's a major.'

'I don't care if he's General Montgomery,' Wilkie said. 'He's not coming sniffing around here.'

And suddenly Iris saw the sense to it, was thankful for Wilkie.

They would all be moving on again now. The war did not stop because people you cared for died and you did not have sufficient time to grieve for them. It was just as well, she thought, sensible at last, there was more to be done and she was glad of it.

Jack escaped to the south and his work. He didn't want to go back to Durham, it would have been so much easier not to but the coward in him didn't win in the end, he kept going back, not as often as he should have but as often as he could bear.

He thought it would get easier but it didn't and he made himself go to see Nan because he knew that however hard it was for him it was just as bad if not worse for her. And through it all he remembered how he had felt after Anna died. Nan would be feeling just like that, like there was nothing left, no way to go forward except through her children and that would carry her on.

It would do no good to suggest as other people did that she would marry again, that she would be happy once more, that she would 'get over it' as they said. He hated that. Nan had loved his son as a man should be loved and should be glad to be loved, not as Iris Black had done. Nan had loved Johnny wholeheartedly and Nan should never know that Johnny had been unfaithful to her, not if he could help it.

He travelled north, he saw Nan, he stood the company of the boys and her sorrow and her mother for as long as he could and then he retreated into town, parked his car outside the County and strode into the bar.

There he ordered a double malt whisky and tried not to down it too quickly. He was known there, he could not let people think badly of him and he knew, though he had his back turned to the room, that people were watching. They always did. No doubt they marvelled at the man who made guns whose son had died in war. Nobody would approach him, nobody would dare.

So he was the more surprised when someone said his name. He looked up and a young man was standing there, looking clearly at him.

'Mr Fenwick? You don't know me. I'm David Black.'

Jack stared at him for a few seconds.

'I don't want to disturb you,' David said,

'but I couldn't sit just across the room and not come over and tell you how sorry I am that Johnny has died. I know that my parents were very fond of him and always wished Iris had married him. She was so ungovernable, you know.'

The lad's courage and his maturity and his kind words made Jack smile.

'Can I get you a drink?'

'I don't like to intrude.'

'Oh, please. I have enough of my own company.' And in a lot of ways it was comforting having Iris's brother there. He looked nothing like her other than a vague family resemblance and the same green eyes. 'Sit down. What would you like?'

'I'll have what you're having.'

'Good choice,' Jack said and ordering David's drink he was able to order himself another.

They talked about work which was what they had in common and it was easy because they knew a great many of the same people and Jack had met David's father at various industrial conferences and gatherings and although the foundry was very small and as business people they were unimportant it didn't matter. The war was a common cause and Jack was local enough to be aware of everything that was happening.

'How's Iris?' Jack found he could ask after his second drink.

'We don't hear much from her. She's in France now. I know that she was very upset when Johnny died.'

'She's ... very special.'

'She's very hard work,' David said and made him smile again. 'My parents are looking forward to having her home when the war ends but goodness only knows what she will do next.'

'I'm sure she'll think of something nobody ever envisaged,' Jack said.

It hurt to think of Iris, it hurt to talk of her almost as much as it hurt not to and the guilt over the way that he had felt about her came down on Jack like a blanket. He almost wished he had not asked except that it gave him back that picture of her standing in the early morning at the castle, bare-legged, wearing a white shirt and then talking to him as though they were old friends over tea and toast and honey. It was one of the happiest memories of his life and he held on to it because he could not bear to think that his son would never walk in the door again. The war would finish for some people. For others it would last a lifetime.

Fourteen

Iris had dreamed of coming back, had gone over it in her mind so many times that it could never live up to her expectations, she thought. The war was finally over and she had ended it in France where she had begun. She was tired now as she had never been tired in her life. Every bone ached, every muscle. She had been on the way for so very long and now her heart beat hard as the train pulled into Durham station.

It made her want to laugh. She could see so little. It was cold, dark, raining just like it so often was in early summer and all that was visible of the small city she had always loved so much, and never more so than now when she had been away from it for so long, was tiny little chinks of light, slivers of cream which crept from under and to the sides of the curtains where people huddled over their fires.

She collected her baggage, such as it was, slight and shabby, and then stepped down on to the platform. The train pulled away and as it did so a rather fat woman in a beaver lamb coat ran the few yards between them and drew Iris into an embrace she recognized

194

well and she was transported back to her childhood, the smell of lavender water, the way that the fur went up her nose, the hard chink of her mother's pearls and the warmth such as no other person had ever given her.

She was in the certain embrace of her mother's arms, she felt the assurance of her mother's love. Her mother's only sister had died in the war and Iris could not imagine how that would feel. She was all the more glad to be able to come back, to reassure her mother that such things could happen.

'We expected you weeks ago.'

'I know. There was a lot to do,' Iris said.

Her father was there too, not as tall as she remembered, rather more stooping, in a long dark coat, buttoned against the weather. He smelled of tobacco and his hand was cold as his fingers caressed her cheek and finally David, much taller even than she remembered, slender and rather awkward, bumping her against him as though they were unfamiliar and he didn't know how to treat her.

David carried her luggage and they walked down to where the big silver Bentley was parked and then she was really home and it was difficult not to cry because it had exceeded her expectations.

David drove, her father sat in the front passenger seat, her mother sat with her in the back, holding her hand in fear, Iris thought, that she should prove not to be real and might disappear into the night.

So many women were not coming home, Iris was aware of it. How many mothers could not clasp their daughters' hands? How many nurses had been raped, tortured, shot, blown up, starved and worked to death by the Japanese? She tried not to think about it too much, had told herself she owed it to them to get on with the rest of her life but she did not want to be disrespectful either to the memory of her friends or to the many other women who had given their lives in the war.

And Johnny. Johnny would never come back to Durham. There would be no homecoming of any kind for so many people. She tried not to think about him all the time but he was there alongside every thought, like a ghost or a shadow.

She would never be free of him. She did not want to be in some ways. In other ways she wished she did not dream of him while she slept or long for him with her whole mind and body while she was awake. Durham without Johnny. Was it a thought not to be borne?

It was raining when Wilkie got home. She had been on the move for so long, had envisaged for so many days what this would be like that it was strange when the dream turned into reality. She got off the bus, hauling her luggage after her, and began to walk up the deserted street towards home and it was only then that she put down her luggage and cried.

She didn't know why. How many times had this been her last thought before she went to sleep, how many times had she said reassuring words to a boy who was dying, had talked to him of home, of his parents, of the things she missed most, like being a child and playing in the street and of his mother calling his name down the back when it was time for bed in the evening gloom?

She picked up her bags and told herself that it was only because she was weary, and she continued what she had supposed was a short distance before she reached the back lane.

The lane was unmade and rough and there were big puddles. She skirted around them carefully in the darkness, remembering as she walked where they were and every now and then a light gleamed in a back room window.

She found their yard gate and pushed it open and the back door was unlocked as always, the light was burning in there and the goods for sale were laid out on the table. She opened the door and heard her mother's voice from the front room.

'Is that you, our Wilkie?'

Wilkie thought it was the most wonderful sentence anybody had ever uttered though how her mother knew it was not somebody shopping late she did not know. She thankfully put down her burdens, clashed shut the door and said, 'Aye, it's me,' and her mother came up the step which led to the pantry and the outside door and hugged her.

'Oh,' she said, 'I'm so glad to see you back.'

Wilkie went with her into the front room to the fire, roaring big and red and orange as she had remembered.

'Where's Dad?'

Her mother hesitated.

'Upstairs. He isn't well.'

This was nothing new. Her dad had been poorly for as long as she could remember but for him to be upstairs was not a good sign.

'Go up to him. I'll make you some tea.'

Wilkie climbed the steep stairs and her father heard her and she could hear the joy in his voice when he said,

'Is that my lass?'

'Who else would it be at this time of night?' she said, pushing open the door.

A small fire burned in the grate. She did not remember having seen such a thing before. Her mother should not be carrying coal buckets up the stairs was her first thought. Then she looked at her father.

Wilkie had seen too many men dying not to acknowledge to herself with a kind of sickening thud that her father would not live much longer. She sat down on the bed and let him take her into his arms. They were thin and white and so was his face.

'You've been gone so long,' he said.

'I'm here now and I'm not going away again.'

'Your mother needs the help,' he said and all the ideas that she had had of coming back and taking up another nursing post, of perhaps even having a little house of her own, were quenched in those moments.

'We did worry about you,' he said.

'There was never any need.'

'We're proud of you, you know. I knew you had it in you, you were always made of stern stuff.'

He didn't say 'not like our Joyce'. He had not, as far as she could remember, ever compared either of them to the other or to their mother.

Her mother brought the tea up on a tray and they sat companionably over the fire when he had fallen asleep.

'How's Joyce?' Wilkie did not want to ask but she knew that she ought.

'She should never have married that man,' her mother said. 'He's not a Christian at all, isn't George. He doesn't ask us there and we don't like to go because we know he doesn't want us and he won't let her come here. She isn't happy but then–' she glanced at her husband's sleeping form – 'how long do you think he's got?'

'What did the doctor say?' Wilkie asked, tactfully.

'Oh, they never tell you anything. They wanted him in hospital but he wouldn't hear of it. He says he wants to die in his own bed.'

It was more than millions of people had done during the war and her father was an old man in comparison to them, Wilkie told herself, though it was of little comfort. Looking closer at her mother for the first time she thought she wasn't too good either, her lined face, tired eyes and bent form told the other side of the story. The arthritis which she had had for years had got worse. Her left hand was twisted, the fingers bent from shape and the right was swollen badly between thumb and fingers.

'I'm here now,' Wilkie said. 'I'll look after you.'

'You'll want to go into nursing, as soon as you get yourself rested. It's what you're trained for,' her mother said.

'Later,' Wilkie said.

David had altered so much, Iris did not know why. He was even quieter than she remembered. She thought this was just because they had not seen one another in so long and it was frustrating.

'How are you?' she said when they sat by themselves in the late evening by the fire.

'Fine. How are you managing without Johnny?'

'It's been such a long time now. I think I'm beginning to get used to it. What about you? Anybody special?'

She expected him to laugh, brush it off but he didn't. He said awkwardly,

'As a matter of fact there is.'

Iris felt cool surprise.

'Really?'

'Ella Welsh.'

Iris thought for a moment.

'I don't think I know her.'

'Yes, you do.'

'Do you mean Ella Armstrong?'

'That's right.'

'She used to run the cafe on Silver Street.'

'I've asked her to marry me.'

Iris's lips felt like rubber. How awful of her to be jealous and not just because Ella would get in the way of her relationship with her brother but because she was alone. Ella and David would have one another and she had nobody.

Their meeting was even less promising. Ella was chocolate-box pretty, she had glossy dark hair and china-blue eyes and Iris could not imagine why David had chosen her above all the girls he could have chosen to be his wife. She was so ordinary, did not have any interesting conversation, like somebody who had never been out of Durham. Ella did not even look particularly pleased to be there in the sitting room at Iris's house.

She kept glancing nervously towards the door and was happier when Iris's parents were there. Iris could not think what it must be like to lose your family home after several hundred years. Swan Island was – by repute, she had never seen it – the most beautiful house in the area and because Ella's father had been profligate with what his family had proudly owned for so long they had lost it and he had killed himself.

Ella had spent most of her life in dark narrow quarters above the Silver Street cafe and Iris didn't envy her that. She knew also that Ella had been briefly married to Jack Welsh in the early part of the war and that he had died tragically in training. Perhaps she was still in love with him.

She certainly didn't look at David the way a woman who loved him would have, Iris thought. Perhaps David was just a way of leaving a horrid life behind her. Certainly he was a big step up for her and most women would have given a great deal to leave behind a few squalid little rooms and a life of getting up at the crack of dawn to make pastries.

As to David, Iris had never seen him in love before. He was besotted. Her parents, she could see, liked Ella. They hugged her as she came into the house.

Iris was surprised though, when Ella said to her later, as they had a little privacy for the first time by the sitting-room fire, 'I wondered whether you would be my bridesmaid. I have no sister of my own.'

Iris stared at her. Did Ella have no tact at all or did she not know about Johnny and would it matter anyhow?

She wanted to say, 'I would rather not,' but couldn't.

She made herself smile. She said that she would be delighted. Ella looked relieved rather than pleased.

Iris thought back to all her friends, the women she had met during the war. They were scattered. Many of them she had not heard from since. It was too difficult to make a friend of Ella when Ella did not understand the war.

What a strange thing to ask somebody you had never met before, as though they were nominated even though you might dislike them? It had obviously not occurred to Ella that Iris might dislike her. What conceit. Perhaps she was short of friends and had nobody but her fiancé's sister to ask.

'The wedding is soon, then?' That too was a shock. She hadn't realized when she came home that one of the first things she would be called upon to do was attend her only brother's wedding.

'Oh, yes, next month. Nothing big of

course. I have no family and ... your father has bought us a house in the bailey.'

'That was nice of him. North or South?' Iris said.

Her sarcasm was not lost, she could see, on her almost sister-in-law.

'Not far up from the river,' Ella said, holding her eyes with her own sparking gaze. 'You will do it, then? We'll have to make do and mend for dresses of course.'

'I'm sure my mother will conjure something suitable. She comes from a family of very good dressmakers and we have plenty of old dresses. Is she making something for you?' Iris asked sweetly.

'I'm wearing my mother's wedding dress.'

Let's hope it brings you more luck than it did for her, Iris said silently.

Ella tried on the dress. While elegant it was very unfashionable with a full-length lace veil which Iris thought hideous. It was heavy satin, beaded with a low waistline, and had gone cream at the edges.

'Are you dedicated to the idea of wearing it?' Iris could not help saying.

'Do you think I shouldn't?' Ella asked.

'Honestly?'

Ella nodded.

'I think you should have a wedding dress of your own.'

'Things are hard to come by.'

'David ought to be able to arrange something, surely, or if you asked my mother she could probably bring that one up to date.'

'Would she?'

'Certainly she would. Come downstairs,' and when they did so Iris called her mother in from the kitchen.

Lottie looked dubiously at the dress.

'Does it look awful?' Ella ventured.

'It's a bit big for you. If it was taken in a little it could look much better and it could be dyed...' She stopped there. Ella was shaking her head.

'It's very faded,' Iris said.

'Stand there and I'll go and get some pins.'

Fifteen minutes later the dress looked much better when it was fitted well to Ella's slender figure.

'There, how is that?' Lottie said.

'Oh, I like it,' Ella said.

On the morning of the wedding Ella looked so pale that Iris said impishly, 'You aren't pregnant, are you?'

Ella went whiter, if that were possible. And then for the first time ever Iris felt sympathy and affection for the other woman and said softly, 'Oh, I'm sorry, it was meant to be a joke. You aren't, though?'

'No, of course not,' Ella said stiffly, and then she tried a smile and Iris could see the tears were close. 'I just wish my mother was here, or my grandmother at least.'

'You'll have to put up with me and my mother. She's very nice. I'm not of course any more, if I ever was. Are you thinking about your first wedding?'

Ella put a hand on her arm and said with a glimpse of humour, 'I'm hoping it's going to be much better than that.'

Iris, rather pleased with this response, could not help a giggle.

'At least you've got to the altar twice. I haven't managed it at all so far.'

'Somebody will take you on,' Ella said and the tears receded.

'You look beautiful,' Iris said and it was true. 'And David is very nice, I can say that even though he's my brother. I'm sure you'll be happy.'

'I do hope so.'

Ella was married from their house for she had nowhere else to be married from and nobody to be married from either but it didn't matter. It was, without doubt, the best wedding Iris had ever been to in spite of the fact that she felt she was losing her brother. It was the idea of celebration at the end of so many years of war. It felt like going forward at last.

'I wanted to have a word with you about the wedding,' David said.

'Oh, why?' Iris said. 'You don't want me to

be best man as well as the bridesmaid, do you?'

David smiled patiently.

'I've invited Jack Fenwick,' he said.

'Johnny's father? Whatever for?'

'He's taken to spending time in the area since the war finished. I just thought I should tell you.'

Iris was suddenly alarmed as she thought of the day that they had met and how kind he had been and of how he must feel about the loss of his son. 'Has he married again?' she asked.

'No.'

'I thought he might. Men are so desperate for sons,' Iris said.

It was wrong and would have been unsubtle to crane her neck in the church on the day of the wedding. She did not see him in the church but then everybody who had been invited had come. People were in need of some kind of hope for the future and what better than a wedding.

Many items were still rationed but everyone did what they could and although it was a somewhat subdued affair foodwise her father had contributed a great number of bottles of champagne which he had been keeping for many years for such an occasion so he said, so that the first thing they all did was to have a glass and the noise of people enjoying themselves rose like a wave.

It was then that she saw Jack Fenwick standing alone in the middle of the sitting room. People kept going up to him, speaking briefly and then coming away. Iris didn't want to talk to him but it would have been cowardly. She had lost the love of her life but he had lost his only child so when there was a space around him and watching the many women there eyeing him Iris made her way across in a decisive manner which she hoped would deter anyone from getting in her way.

As she got nearer, he looked directly at her. Had his eyes always been so dark, so cold? Iris faltered in her step. He was taller than she remembered and as slender as Johnny had been. His grief sat on him as well as his expensive suit, another layer of impenetrability. She knew now why people were afraid and did not stay near.

This man had built aircraft, ships, tanks, guns. He was rich through war. When men killed one another he prospered. Companies like his had been responsible for the arming of the Allies and because of them the war had been won but also because of such things his child had died. Iris forgot how nervous she was and smiled.

'Mr Fenwick. Hello.'

'Miss Black, and wearing much more than the last time I saw you.' If any of her father's friends had said such a thing she would have been offended but he spoke so lightly and his eyes were not quite as glacial somehow.

For the first, time in months Iris felt like a woman. She laughed.

'Isn't it hideous?' she said, indicating the long blue gown. 'My mother made it from something she had in the attic.'

His dark eyes danced. Iris thought she could go on looking into them for ever.

'I shan't ask you how you are,' she said. 'I'm so very sorry about Johnny.' She hesitated there, stopped and he said,

'Please go on. I love to hear my son's name on other people's lips.'

'I nursed him,' she said.

'Did you really? I'm so glad.'

Iris was about to give him the nurse's spiel about how he died without pain and quickly and how Johnny had spoken of his father before he died but Jack Fenwick's mouth stopped her. It tightened ever so slightly though his eyes didn't shift.

'And I cared very much for him.'

Jack Fenwick made no comment to that and to Iris's relief the meal was ready then and they sat down to eat. He was nowhere near but she could see him from where she was sitting, smiling just a little at people and doubtlessly making polite conversation, lingering in the dining room where people were smoking, drinking coffee and chatting.

Later there was music and dancing, her

brother having friends who were in a band and the carpet having been put into the garage. The sitting room was big and soon full of those who wanted to dance. Jack Fenwick had disappeared. Iris thought he had gone home but she found him in the little sitting room at the back of the house, alone over whisky and a cigarette.

'Don't you ever ask anyone to dance?' she said, sitting on the arm of the sofa beside his chair.

He eyed her narrowly.

'Well?' Iris prompted.

He flicked the ash off his cigarette into the glass ashtray on the table in front of him and said,

'I don't dance.'

'Would you like another drink?'

'I would like it if you left me alone.'

'Why did you come?'

'What?' She had his attention now.

'Why did you come to the wedding? You're noted for your unsociable behaviour. You could have refused. I hear you never go anywhere.'

'You know nothing about me.'

'Yes, I do.'

'Iris...' he said and stopped.

'What?'

Iris took a swig of the gin and tonic which she held in her hand. He didn't answer and she felt brave.

'Did you ever consider getting married again?' she said.

He smiled, rather in spite of his mood and without looking beyond the cigarette.

'Is this a proposal?' he said.

'There have been times when I wished I had married Johnny.'

'It wasn't like that,' Jack said.

She was taken aback.

'How do you know?'

'It was an affair,' he said, 'it was never going to be anything else.'

'You being an expert at these matters.'

'Nan was the right woman for him to marry.'

'And I was the right woman for him to screw, is that it?'

Any respectable man would have exploded with anger at that point, at her insinuation, at her language, she thought. The least of men would have glanced around to make sure nobody was in the hall or within hearing range.

Jack Fenwick took a sip of whisky and said, 'Would you like a cigarette?'

She took one. He lit it for her from a silver lighter and then one for himself.

'After Dunkirk,' Iris said, 'we spent the night in York. When I was in Egypt I thought about it such a lot, the hotel with the pretty garden, the meal they put in front of us in such hard times, the bottle of wine. When things were really bad I would think about it every night, fall asleep thinking about it. Nan had his children and I had a night in York.'

'It was what you wanted.'

'I suppose it was,' Iris allowed and she finished her drink.

One of David's friends, a young man who owned some kind of factory and thought that because of it he was a gift to the world, came into the room and said to her, 'Why are you sitting here when you could be dancing with me?'

Iris saw the secret smile form on Jack Fenwick's mouth. He obviously thought he was going to get rid of her.

'Too late,' she said, 'Mr Fenwick has just asked me.'

The evening was advanced by then and the dancing was slow. Iris's first thought was that she would rather her parents didn't see her in Jack Fenwick's arms. The lights were dimmed, the floor was not so full that people would not notice. She only hoped he wouldn't hold her too close. It would look so bad and besides which she had no desire to be held close by a middle-aged man.

This concept lasted for about thirty seconds because Johnny's father held her no closer than he should. Nobody could have faulted him except that Iris did because in those seconds her body clamoured to be nearer.

The voice which told her she was being ridiculous was drowned out by the screaming hunger which would have made a tidal wave look soft upon a beach. She was disgusted with herself and wanted to burst into tears.

When the music stopped he said, 'Thank you, Miss Black, for doing an old man such a kindness,' and he walked out of the room.

It was very late when the Black family went to bed. Iris had danced with half a dozen young men by then, all of them married, all of them being polite. She was only thankful to reach her room, just to find moments later a brief knocking on the door and her mother coming in. Iris thought she wanted to talk about Ella and David but she could see by her mother's expression that it was not to be.

'Iris, you're a grown woman and you've been through a great deal, more than I have, more than most women have, so I hope you won't take this amiss but whatever are you doing with that man?'

Iris concentrated on taking off her pearls and went on looking in the mirror at her reflection, wishing she did not look so old.

'What man?' she said.

Her mother sat down on the bed.

'Oh, Iris,' she said, 'he won't marry you. They say he's devoted to the memory of his dead wife and Lord knows every woman in the area has thrown either her unmarried sister or her daughter at him and I'm not saying that he's ever done anything he shouldn't but ... he's dangerous.'

Iris laughed.

'Mother,' she said.

'I saw you with him. You like him.'

'I do like him,' Iris said, realizing it.

'He's at least twenty years older than you.'

'Yes, but you must admit he's very sexy,' Iris said, going over and kissing her.

Her mother tried to laugh.

'Don't be silly, dear,' she said. 'Is this because of Johnny?'

'No, no,' Iris said. Only it was. Maybe it had something to do with them both having been so close to him, knowing him as few people ever had, as nobody now ever would.

'They ennobled Jack Fenwick, you know. He's Lord Fenwick.'

'And you think I want to be Lady Fenwick? I don't. Don't worry.'

Her mother shook her head.

'I'm afraid you will do something worse,' she said. 'He will never marry, Iris, not you and not anybody. You won't get involved with him, will you?'

'Of course not. I don't suppose he spends any time here. He's probably going back to London,' Iris said.

And it was true, so the reports said in the weeks that followed. He had nothing to stay there for now, Iris knew.

Fifteen

Wilkie had taken to sitting up at night with her father. She doubted she would ever be tired again. She could serve in the shop all day and in the early evening while Bess dozed over the front-room fire she would go up and spend her time talking softly to his sleeping form or gazing from the window at the houses across the street.

People did not always close their curtains and she could see them sitting around the fire as the autumn turned into winter and she wondered what it was like to have a man to come home to you, to make a meal, the smell of egg and chips, or meat pies with gravy, and she would watch the lights go out downstairs when the evening wore on and then the upstairs curtains being pulled across and she thought of people warm in bed and then she would turn from the window.

Having seen so many men die did not make watching her father do so any better. None of those men had ever looked upon her school reports with pride, walked across the snowy fields towards the town, put a hand on her shoulder as they walked around in the sweet gloom of the cathedral on a cold afternoon.

On Sundays if she opened the bedroom window her father fancied he could hear the bells calling people in for evensong, the choir singing the Magnificat, their voices lifted as night fell upon the city.

She could never hear anything but she was pleased for him. All she heard was his breathing, hoarse and laboured. Iris wrote, asking to see her but Wilkie ignored the letters. She replied politely that they could not come to Ella and David's wedding and she knew that it sounded rude after what his parents had done for Joyce and George when they were getting married but the truth of the matter was that Wilkie knew by experience that she could bear a great many things in her life but she could not stand there and watch David Black marry his sweetheart.

It was nothing personal, it was not that she had ever in a thousand years imagined that such a man would glance in her direction but she considered it particularly cruel of God that she should be acquainted with him. She could not do it, she could not explain, she said that her father was not well enough to leave the house, her mother would not go without him and she did not like to leave her mother but she stressed to Iris that she did not want visitors.

Iris might think it rude. Wilkie was beyond

caring. On the day that David and Ella were married she went on as normal and it took every bit of strength she had to do it. That night she fell asleep in the chair in her father's room and dreamed that she was running far away and when she awoke it was the day after the wedding and she thought that nothing would ever be as difficult again.

She did not let anything or anyone intrude on her father's final days that winter. She did not want possibly the last day to be sullied with the sound of other people's voices. Joyce came, usually when George was out visiting the members of his parish but never on Sundays because then Joyce was required at the church, sitting in the front pew, her and George's children in a line, their faces lifted up as George preached the sermon, like eyes unto the hills, Wilkie thought savagely.

George did not come to see her father or her mother. Joyce often talked about the war and how it had been one of the easiest most peaceful times of her life. The bombs might fall, the country might be taken by the Hun but Joyce had been happy at home with her mother and father, in the small sure world which Heath Houses provided for her.

Wilkie had not wished George ill but she could not understand how George had had what people called 'a good war'. Not for him wounded or suffering. George had come through unscathed, the only person she knew who was unchanged, and there was a great deal which needed to be changed, Wilkie thought.

Iris determined to go and see Wilkie. They hadn't been in touch since the end of the war and Iris did not like to go unannounced but she missed her. She trudged up the long narrow road and found the shop. When she went in the bell tinkled and the curtain which led into the front of the house was pushed aside and there stood Wilkie, looking just the same as she had always looked, broad, red-faced, jolly, like somebody who lived in the country.

They hugged and Wilkie said how glad she was to see her and then took her into the other room to see her mother. The older lady was not well, Iris could soon see, and there was no sign of her father. The day had darkened with rain. The rain poured down the small sash window, engulfing the place in gloom, and they sat over the meagre fire.

The little sofa was lumpy and uncomfortable, the floor was covered in green linoleum. They drank their tea and talked about their war and the people they had known and from time to time Wilkie got up and went into the shop to serve customers.

When Wilkie's mother fell asleep over the fire Iris ventured, 'What happened to your father?'

'He died a little while since. He had been ailing for a long time, you know. He had an accident down the pit and was never right after that.'

'How awful. I'm sorry, I didn't know he had died. You should have told me. I would have helped. I would have come to the funeral.'

'I didn't want anybody else involved somehow,' Wilkie said, not looking at her. 'I didn't think I'd be stuck here keeping the shop, such as it is.'

'Did you not think of going back to nursing?'

'Not while Mother isn't well.'

'You could leave her with someone. It would pay much better.'

'I know but I can't do that to her. She hates being left and I've been away such a long time and she doesn't often see Joyce.'

'What a difficult life you lead.'

'It was awful to come back to after we had gone through such a lot. I'd hardly seen my dad for years. He was a lovely man, you know, Iris. I do miss him. He was clever. If he'd ever had chance or education he would have gone far. He taught me to play chess when I was really little and he loved us all so much. He never said he would rather we had been boys and if we had been we could have gone down the pit and brought real money home.'

'You did bring real money home when you nursed and I'm sure it's as hard as any pit job.'

Wilkie smiled.

'I like the way you defend the people you care about, Iris.'

'I shall always care about you and Joyce. Could you not go and live with them? They must have lots of room.'

Wilkie looked scathingly at her.

'George wouldn't have us in his huge vicarage. He doesn't like me and I can't say I care for him so he never comes here.'

'I wish he was a more sensitive man.'

'After what we did to him?'

'There was nothing else for Joyce to do. She couldn't come home.'

'She should have got rid of it,' Wilkie said. 'We would have helped her.'

'Maybe we should have. It didn't seem like the right thing to do at the time and I don't think she would ever have agreed.'

'Where are they?'

'Back in Durham. George has the parish just the other side of the city. I thought that would help, you know, but it doesn't. I think George has got worse with keep and they have three children now. She looks awful. I feel so guilty about their marriage, I don't think it's working well.'

'I feel guilty about it too but I don't see what else we could have done.'

'She was so stupid.'

'A lot of other women have been the same.'

'And now we're supposed to be grateful because we've come through the war,' Wilkie said savagely.

'I am grateful,' Iris said but she shuddered. 'I ought to go and see her.'

'I don't think you should,' Wilkie said. 'It just makes things worse for her. He doesn't seem to want her to have any friends.'

Sixteen

'I don't understand why we should move from here,' Iris said to her parents one early spring morning not long after Ella and David's first child had been born and her father had suggested that David should have the big house.

Sunlight was pouring into the dining room as they ate breakfast. It was bacon and scrambled eggs, her father's favourite on Sundays. They both looked up, staring at her.

'It's what my parents did for us,' her father said.

'Yes, but it was your house,' Iris pointed out, 'you bought it and they lived in it. We are three adults. Ella and David have one small child. Why can't they go on living where they are and leave us in peace here? I would like some time to enjoy my home, I was away from it for six years.'

'It's the essence of the thing,' her father said.

'What essence would that be?' Iris insisted.

'You don't understand,' her mother said.

'No, I don't. This is my home. Why should I move out because David is married and has a child?'

'He will probably have several,' her mother said.

'If I had married and had children first would you and David have moved out?'

'That would be different,' her mother said.

'Why would it?'

'David is running the works,' her father said wearily as though tired of her and the subject.

'Hardly logical,' Iris said.

'The house in the bailey is pretty,' her mother said, 'and it will be so much easier to manage.'

'And how will everything fit in?'

'I thought we'd leave most of it here for Ella and David,' her mother said.

Iris thought of the old furniture, much of it Edwardian. She thought of the oak desk in her bedroom which stood in front of the window. She thought of how big that bedroom was. It had been hers for as long as she could remember. She did not see why she should give things up when Ella and David had so much and she had so little.

She would have argued but stopped herself because her mother had gone pale and her father looked so tired and worn. They had been a shock to her when she came home, they seemed so much older as though the whole thing had been too much for them.

Her mother missed her sister even though she had lived in London for years and they had hardly seen her, Iris's father had been overworked all the time and they had had a great deal to endure what with the work and her being away and the worry.

She would have fought long and hard to stay here but it was not fair to her parents, she knew it wasn't. It was not her house, after all, she owned nothing. It pained her to think of it. She had no rights of ownership nor of any other kind.

She was only the daughter. David was the son, he would carry things on, he had a little boy, he had already established the next generation and because of it they had awarded him this house which she loved so much, had longed to come back to and was now about to lose to a horrid little house which held no good memories of her childhood.

She wanted to say that she ached for some peace, she had dreamed about this house when she was away and it was all true but it would not make the difference.

There was no point in arguing, her father had made up his mind and making things difficult would not change anything, she knew. She hated moving but there was nothing she could do other than resent David for the first time in her life, he was so important, she was nobody.

He did not understand, did not care how she felt. Nothing mattered to him now other than Ella and their baby. That was what men were like, Iris thought bitterly, they married and then their families essentially lost them.

The house in the bailey which had been her parents' wedding present to David and Ella was tiny by comparison to her home and it got no light. At one side it had a long narrow garden and beyond that was the river and the sitting room and her parents' bedroom faced that way but Iris's bedroom, the only other of any size, overlooked the cobbled street which dropped narrowly to the cathedral gardens and then beyond to the river which went around in a loop and on to Framwellgate. She tried not to hate it and not to feel bitter towards Ella and David but they seemed to have everything and were not even conscious of it.

Sometimes at night Iris would lie in her bed and hear the drift of young people's voices, students, as they came home, girls laughing and light-footed, boys with deeper tones and heavier steps. She thought of all the boys and girls who had died, whose voices would never be heard again, many like Johnny, buried in far-off lands, since it was impractical to bring their bodies home. How quickly people forgot the sacrifices which had been made, how little anyone soon seemed to care.

Across the bailey were other houses and in the early evenings as it grew dark the curtains would be open and she would see families sitting around the dining table or over the fire, children on the hearthrug, parents in wing chairs, listening to the wireless.

The calm after the storm, she thought, survivors of the war. How lucky they were, how much they had. She considered it her duty to try and go on when so many had died but she had not understood that it would be so hard.

She hated her single bed. The room was big enough for a double but her mother had left all the double beds except for one. Iris hated the assumption that because you weren't married anything would do.

She thought back to the bedroom she had had in the old house, the way the little writing desk had stood at the window and the two little bookcases at either side of the double bed. She thought of the pretty dressing table with the big mirrors and the wardrobe.

It all went together and since it would not fit here it had been left. What she had now was bits and pieces as though neither she nor the furniture mattered. Her mother and father didn't care any more. Her mother had looked so pleased to leave the big house to Ella and David.

Her father wasn't well. He was always falling asleep in his chair over the fire. He did not want to do anything and if Iris suggested to her mother that they might go shopping or for a walk her mother always said that she did not like to leave him.

They had help. It was the only good thing. Mrs Pearson came in twice a week to clean and do the washing. Iris did the shopping, the cooking, the washing-up, most of the ironing, the general tidying around, even the garden, and she looked after her parents. She had thought she would go back to nursing whereas in fact she had quite enough to do.

She had no money other than her savings which was her pay from the war. Her parents did not seem to think she needed any. Not that they were mean. Her father gave her the housekeeping because she did the food shopping and he was generous. Her mother paid for her clothes. For anything else she knew she had only to ask. It was the having to ask which Iris disliked most. She was so aware of being the unmarried daughter. She was 'Miss Black'. She came to loathe it.

I wanted my freedom so badly, Iris thought, and now that I have it there seems nowhere I want to go, nobody I want to go with, nobody who wants to go with me. How strange, dreaming of how something will be and finding it quite different.

Halfway up Saddler Street one crisp day, snow falling, Iris saw Nan Fenwick across the road. She had two boys with her, one tall, one younger, smaller. Johnny's sons. Iris made herself look away for fear that they should be the image of him but she could not help wondering why women were obliged to make such hard choices.

Given enough time, she thought, maybe we would have been able to have both and then she thought, no, we wouldn't. I was nursing and Johnny was soldiering and there was not enough time so in a way it was the best for all of us, as it worked out.

But then, Johnny had not seen his sons grow up, would never enjoy their successes, help with their difficulties, or see his grand-children.

The street seemed full of couples at that point except Nan at one side, pale, serious-faced, widowed, and she at the other, single and lonely. A spinster, an old maid. And then she thought back to the nights with Johnny, to the sweetness of his body, and the pleasure. Not many old maids about any more, she thought and she was still smiling when she opened the front door of the house in the bailey.

It was three days later and she was in her room when her mother came up the stairs with a curious expression on her face.

'Johnny Fenwick's wife is here,' she said.

'What, Nan?' Iris said, as though it could be anybody else.

'I put her in the sitting room,' her mother said as if Nan was an important parcel.

His wife, Iris thought as she made her way down the stairs. Perhaps her mother did not think of Nan as a widow or perhaps she just didn't want to. She opened the door carefully. Nan was skinny, she had never put on weight and now she was pale with shadows beneath her eyes.

'Nan,' Iris said, with forced gaiety, 'how are you?'

'Hello, Iris.'

They had never been friends so it wasn't easy. She had been comparatively rich and Nan had had nothing, and rich and poor did not mix. Nan had seemed dull, badly dressed, tongue-tied when they were young and Iris could have chosen to make a friend of her and helped but she had not and it felt uncomfortable now.

She knew enough to be sorry that they could not and would not be friends and worse still she remembered after Dunkirk how she and Johnny had gone off together when he should have been coming home to his wife and children.

She was very ashamed of them both. It had mattered so much to her – she found herself clinging to that memory more than any of the others – and it was hard to meet Nan's eyes.

'I thought I saw you across the road the other day but I wasn't sure and I had both the boys with me so...' Nan said.

'Yes, I saw you too. I didn't know what to say.'

'You saw Johnny before he died.'

It wasn't quite a question and Iris got ready, as nurses always did, to assure Nan that Johnny had not felt any pain, that he had died in his sleep or very soon after he was hurt or another of the dozen different lies which could be told to relatives to make their grieving less.

She wanted to say that he had not complained, that he had been patient, that she had seen him before he died and although all of these things were true she could not say any of them.

When she didn't answer immediately Nan looked down at her fingers.

'I would have come before but ... somehow I couldn't manage it.'

'Wilkie nursed him, not me.' It seemed important to make sure Nan knew there had been nothing more than the brief contact of friends. 'He spoke of you very fondly and of his sons.'

'Did he?' Nan's clear eyes were the most unnerving part of her, Iris thought. Were they one of the reasons Johnny had married her?

'He told me that he loved you very much and how much he cared for his boys and how he wished he could get back to see them. It was all that mattered to him.' I'll never get to heaven, Iris thought, I'm full of lies.

'He never loved me,' Nan said, her gaze clear and true. 'You were the one he loved. He only married me because you wouldn't have him–'

'That was a very long time ago. Things are different when you're twenty. Besides, if he hadn't wanted to marry you why would he have, you had no money, no social graces?'

The seeming brutality made Nan smile and Iris was just glad you could divert her.

'I was so poor, so ... needy.'

'Your boys are handsome, just like him, and he loved you all and missed you and wished he could have seen you again. I'm sorry for you, Nan, you must miss him dreadfully.'

Nan didn't say anything for what felt to Iris like minutes and could only have been a few seconds.

'I came here to give you something I thought you might like to have.' She fished from her large black handbag a very expensive gold wristwatch which Iris could remember him wearing when they had stayed together at the castle. 'His father gave him this for his twenty-first birthday. I would like you to have it.'

'I couldn't possibly do such a thing.' What did Nan want her to do, drown in guilt?

'Please. I know he would have liked it if you would take it. It's not exactly feminine but... Please take it, Iris. You might wear it sometimes.'

When Nan looked at her Iris could see that Nan felt sorry for her which was the best thing she could have made Nan feel so she took the watch, stammered her thanks and as Nan made for the front door Iris began to feel sorry for herself. Nan had his sons and the memories of her marriage. What did she have, a night in York, a few days at the castle in his arms when they were young and the day that Johnny had proposed and she had refused him?

However she wore the watch and it gave her comfort.

Seventeen

Iris would not have been the nurse she was if she had not noticed that her father began to fail. The war had been too much for him, perhaps it had been too much for all of them. He would go to the foundry but she suspected that her brother did the majority of the work.

Not that he ever said anything but occasionally she would go to the office and find David exasperated because his father would not allow him to run things as he chose. It was always behind closed doors. David cared for his father too much to say such things to his face.

'I just wish he would go home a bit earlier,' was the nearest he got to complaining, as they sat in his office one day when she had gone there specifically to talk to him about the situation.

She had had to get past Madeline, his secretary, first. Iris didn't like Madeline, and that was awful, she knew. She didn't like anybody who was close to her brother. How ridiculous and how rude. She wished she could help it but Madeline was attractive, soft voiced and ran David's office with the kind of cool competence Iris would have given much to copy. She wore neat dark-coloured costumes to the office and white blouses, almost like a uniform. It made her look even more efficient than Iris suspected she already was.

Also she should feel sorry for Madeline because Madeline had about her the half-desperate air of a woman who wants a man in her bed and can't have him because he's married and doesn't think of her.

She was convinced Madeline adored David in a stupid way and it made Iris impatient of her. Why didn't Madeline go out and find her own man? Iris longed to tell her that she was swiftly becoming an old maid. Madeline had been there before the war, was her father's secretary. She would have to get a move on if she was to find a husband anywhere at all or was she too loyal in the stupid way some women had, thinking that David couldn't do without her or that the foundry might fall down if she married and left?

'The foundry is his whole life,' David said as they sat down in his office with the door closed, one cold afternoon. Iris had shut it carefully when she came in, she didn't want Madeline to hear what she had to say.

'I know. This is the trouble.'

'What would he do if he retired?'

'We all have to do that some time and I

think that time has come. You must talk to him about it, David.'

'It's easy enough for you to say.'

'What makes you think my life is any easier than anybody else's?' Iris said and then wished she hadn't. Why should David care, why should he think about her?

'Things aren't easy for any of us.'

'I know they aren't.' Iris leaned forward at the other side of the desk, surprised and rather pleased to be David's confidante. She had been sure he talked to Ella about business, now she wondered. 'Why in particular now?' she said.

'I mean financially they aren't easy.'

'How is that?'

'He has given a great deal away.' David spoke carefully as though not certain he should say such things.

'You mean charity?'

'I don't like that word. He helps people, very often unofficially and sometimes when they can't get help anywhere else because they are...'

'Profligate?'

'Unfortunate is the word, I think. He can't stand by and watch people go hungry.'

'Nobody should go hungry, after we fought so hard.'

'They do,' David said shortly. 'He has all the makings of a great man without the wealth to back it up and so...'

'And so the business is suffering.'

'Something like that. Don't say anything,' David added. 'Nobody else must know.'

She wasn't sure whether to be flattered because he was telling her or worried as to how bad things had got. Surely he was exaggerating.

'Have you told Ella this?'

'No, I don't want her worried. And don't say anything to Mother. We have to let him do what he wants.'

'Shall I suggest he goes home now? It is almost six.'

'Is it?' David glanced at his wristwatch. 'See if you can prise him away.'

She managed to persuade her father to go home but she didn't think he looked well and in the middle of the night when she could not sleep she heard her mother's cry. She got out of bed and ran into their room and her father was already unconscious. Iris stood for a few seconds, stunned that it should have happened so quickly and then as she saw her mother's white upset face the nurse that she had been took over.

'Don't worry, Mother, it's going to be all right,' she said and then she rang for the doctor and David.

All the nursing she had done did not make things any better. When it was somebody you cared about you were just as badly off as other people, worse probably because you knew what was going on, you knew what the possibilities were. Her father could die, for the first time she admitted it to herself as she and her mother and David sat in the hospital corridor.

Eventually they were allowed in to see him, told that it was likely he had had a series of small strokes before now and this had been a bigger one but it was probable that he would recover completely. Iris was so relieved.

She could not remove from her mind the idea that her father would be much better when he was at home. There she would be able to look after him. She was so pleased when he was allowed to come home but her mother worried about him leaving the hospital, would they be able to manage, was he not better off where he was for now?

Iris reassured her, she would take the responsibility, her father would be fine, she told her mother they would not let him come home if they were at all concerned. They brought him back.

He was not an easy patient. Was that because he was older, because they were close or because he wanted to be back at work? He was convinced that David was getting everything wrong.

'You have to rest,' she said, tucking him into bed.

'You with your hospital corners,' he complained. 'I can hardly move.'

'Nonsense,' Iris said with a briskness she did not feel.

Sometimes when he slept in the afternoons she would fall asleep herself in the sunlight from the window and hear the cathedral bells across the warmth of Palace Green and listen to the people below the windows making their way up the cobbles in pilgrimage.

She encouraged her mother to go out as much as she could, to her sewing class, to see her friends and often in the evenings her father's friends would come by and sit with him and talk and as he began to get better they would play cards and tell stories and listen to the wireless.

'You don't have to be here all the time,' her mother said but Iris was afraid that if she went anywhere her father would collapse again. She knew it was a stupid idea but she could not rid herself of it.

Several weeks went by, her father began to go downstairs, first for a short while and then for most of the day. He was even talking about going back to work, and then it happened again in the middle of a Sunday afternoon and maddeningly when she was out of the room. She came back in from the kitchen when she heard her mother's cries from the sitting room and she held him in her arms while her mother rang David and he came as quickly as he could.

Iris did not realize she was still sitting on the floor with her father in her arms.

The ambulance came and once again there was the short distance to the hospital with her mother and David. They sat by the bed while the consultant did various tests. Her father was conscious but only just and did not seem to recognize any of them.

'I want to take him home,' Iris said.

Out in the corridor David said,

'They know what they're doing.'

'I know what I'm doing as well.'

'What do you mean by that?'

'If he's going to die I would rather he died at home.'

'Don't you think that's rather selfish? What about Mother?'

'Selfish? Surely she wants him to die in his own bed.'

'The responsibility for taking a man that sick home is huge.'

'They can't stop us from taking him.'

'He's better off here.'

'You mean it's easier for you if he's here.' Iris glared at her brother.

David sighed.

'Let him go, Iris. It's his time.'

'I will never let him go,' Iris said, 'not until he dies. He's my father and I love him.'

'That's not love,' David said.

'We're taking him home. He belongs

there, he'll be better off there and Mother will feel better when he is there,' Iris said and she went to the doctor and told him.

She was not sorry that her father went home. She knew that he would want to die with her mother and herself there and after that she did not leave the house. He was too sick to leave his bed and all day and all night she nursed him. She wished she didn't feel like that but she couldn't wish that he had died because she didn't know how she would go on without him. He had always been there for them. Surely they could give him the time he needed now.

When he finally died he did so in her arms and she was able to kiss him and take her leave of him and say the things she had wanted to say. It was early afternoon, a bright autumn day. She felt the energy leave his body for the last time. She was sorry he had died, sorry for herself and David and most especially for her mother who would be lonely now but she was not sorry he had lived longer than so many people, that her father had known his children, had time with his wife, been successful in his business and the people of Durham would remember him for his goodness to them, for what he had done whenever he could.

He had lived a good life. There was a child in her which wanted to scream with sorrow because she had not thought her father would ever die and leave her here without him. It seemed so selfish of him. He was not old and yet he was so much older than so many of the soldiers she had nursed but she knew that here again was a gap that would not be filled and she had the feeling she would have to go around with the loss of her father and of Johnny and it was like walking around with holes in you. It was selfish of her and she knew it.

What would she do with the love that she had for her father? Where would it go now that he was dead? There seemed nowhere for all her affection and emotion. It hung around her neck like a heavy chain. This, Iris thought, was the bottom of her life. She had no one and nothing any more.

Eighteen

Iris went for long walks every day after her father died. It was the only way she could keep from being depressed. She had already suspected that she and her mother would be obliged to give up the house in the bailey because David had talked to her about the business failing and that the house needed to be sold, but somehow now she was inclined to think he exaggerated and that it was his own shortcomings which caused the problems.

She would walk the riverbanks and try not to think what it would be like having to live with David, Ella and the two children, Clyde was now a little boy and there was a second child, Susan.

One afternoon when she was on the towpath between Framwellgate Bridge and Elvet she saw a young woman coming towards her holding on to the hand of a small child by her side. Two big boys ran in front. She stopped when they met.

'Why, Iris,' she said, her thin face broadening into a smile.

'Joyce.' She had changed so much that it was an effort to remember her. She looked so much older but of course she was.

'I can't believe it's you,' Joyce said. 'George is the vicar of St Philip's and St James', just up the town. We've been there for some time.' She seemed embarrassed that she had not asked Iris there and fussed with the little girl by her side.

'Wilkie told me.'

'This is Claire and the boys are Matthew and Thomas.'

Iris thought Joyce looked tired, drawn, the child, now getting into the pushchair, cried. Iris shepherded them into the nearest teashop, luckily it was situated down by the river, though Joyce protested at the expense. There Iris silenced the boys with lemonade and cake and took the little girl into her arms.

'She's gone to sleep. What an exceptional talent you have, Iris,' Joyce said, moments later.

'Have a sandwich,' Iris said, offering Spam and chutney.

Joyce wolfed two and eyed the chocolate cake.

'Go on,' Iris said.

'I mustn't. George is always telling me how fat I'm getting. And you haven't had any yet.'

'I'm not hungry.'

'You're awfully thin.'

'My father died,' Iris said, 'it ruins your appetite.'

'Oh, I'm so sorry. He'll be badly missed. I'm expecting my fourth baby in five months. It makes you ravenous.'

'I'm sure it does.'

They talked about the days of training. The boys, full of food, went off outside to the nearby swings to play.

'Tell me about your marriage,' Iris urged her. 'How are things?'

Joyce stared into the distance for a few moments and finally said,

'It was a mistake, Iris. If I'd known what he was really like I would never have married him.'

'It can't be that bad and you didn't have much choice,' Iris said, feeling guilty and responsible.

'I keep telling myself that. George is ... oh, don't let's talk about it, it gets me down.'

'We should go over and see Wilkie.'

'George doesn't like me going there. He says Heath Houses is common and a vicar's wife, especially his, shouldn't be seen in such places. I do see her and Mother sometimes of course, I just don't tell him.'

'So much for Christian charity,' Iris said.

Nineteen

Iris and Lottie moved in with David and Ella just before Christmas, as the house in the bailey had to be sold, they needed the money. One of Iris's favourite memories was of David as a very small boy, maybe two or three and she, seven or eight, dancing in the snow on the lawn, of the Salvation Army coming to the house on Christmas morning and her mother letting her choose which carol she would like them to play.

It was always 'Away in a Manger' and she remembered the smiling faces of the Salvation Army people, the women in their poke bonnets, the dark sturdy clothes they wore, the brass instruments they played, glittering in the snow or against the Christmas morning sunshine.

She remembered the smell of the turkey roasting in the Aga, the small mountains of vegetables, Brussels sprouts like green billiard balls, golden yellow turnip with pepper and butter, parsnips browned in the oven, sage-and-onion stuffing which her mother made in a great tureen, pints of gravy, cranberry sauce glistening red in a glass dish, white wine for her parents, shandy for herself and David, Christmas pudding boiled in a big cloth and white sauce heady with brandy.

There were great piles of toys under the enormous tree at the end of the hall, the red and green and gold of the decorations glistened in the sitting room, big fires burned in every room, the snow turned the garden into a white picture and on those cold Christmas nights the black sky, the diamond stars and the outline of the big fir trees at the bottom of the garden, branches heavy with snow, were to her childish eyes perfect. Everything had lost its savour now.

It was strange to give up the house in the bailey. She had not wanted to move out of the big house when she was moving with her parents to make way for David and Ella and now she didn't want to move back in with just her mother. She felt as though she was leaving her father in the house where he had died. Also it would be strange. She had begun to feel as if the house in the bailey was hers, she so much wanted to have a house of her own but she felt as though she must move back into the big house with her mother and not cause more disruption.

It was not fair to leave Ella with David's mother and the children and besides Iris did not know where she wanted to move to or what she wanted to do. She felt as though she was always changing her life, nothing was ever settled, ever completely ordered.

There was Flo, Ella's help, as well as Ella in the kitchen so she would have no role there of any importance, she would just be another pair of hands, another woman in the house. It did not, she thought smiling to herself, suit her sense of importance to be one of many and it felt very odd to think they were starting a new kind of life now that her father was dead.

She felt as though she ought to go out and get a job of some kind but she did not want to go back to nursing, she had done so much and things had moved on so far. She would help by cooking and by trying to be a part of the family as much as she could but it would not be easy.

Out for a walk one day she ventured into St Philip's and St James's, one of the churches she had been brought up with, and sat there in the gloom of early evening with no lights except beside the altar. A man in a dog collar was messing about at the front and eventually he came across. It was George.

'Can I help?' he said pleasantly.

'You don't remember me? I'm Iris Black.'

'Oh, yes, of course. How could I forget?' There was a slight edge to his words. 'I'm sorry about your father.'

Iris looked around her.

'I find churches difficult since the war.'

'Ah, now there we differ. I find them even

more comforting.'

'I can't forgive God for so many things.'

'I'm sure he understands.'

'I'm not certain I want him to understand,' Iris said.

'Your mother sometimes comes here by herself. I think she remembers being here with your father when they were young, so she says, I think this was her parish church when she was a girl. People in the town tell tales of him, how during the twenties and the thirties Depression your father almost beggared himself feeding the town,' George said.

'I don't remember much about it. I suppose when you're young you're self-absorbed.' Iris was suddenly grateful for George's understanding. Did he really know or was he just doing his bit as the vicar? Whatever, she felt almost warm towards him for saying such wonderful things about her splendid father. She missed her father so much.

'He employed people when there was very little work. He set up soup kitchens and local charities. It cost him dearly.'

Iris said nothing and then she looked at him and she said,

'Thank you. Nobody talks to me about him, it was good of you.'

George said, as though thankful to reach another subject,

'Do you have any plans?'

'I don't know what to do now.'

He hesitated and then he said,

'I could use help in the administrative sense. I don't pay, mind you.'

'I know nothing about such things.'

'You could go to evening classes and learn and while you're learning you could practise here.'

It seemed a sensible suggestion and Iris, sure that her mother would be pleased, agreed.

The vicarage was enormous. It was one thing, Iris discovered, to live in a big house that you could afford to heat, light and furnish. It was quite another when you had no money. Why on earth had the Victorians built such places to house their clergy when they did not pay them enough to warrant it?

Joyce and the children were building a snowman. Iris did not envy her. She was sitting in the little office working and finished the accounts just as Joyce came in, the eldest boy, Matthew, complaining of how cold his fingers were. Joyce put her head round the door.

'Do you fancy a cuppa?' she said.

Iris smiled, put down her pen and followed through into the kitchen, Joyce having divested herself and the children of coats, hats, scarves, gloves and Wellingtons. In the kitchen was a big cream Aga so that at least that room was warm.

'You have a lovely stove,' Iris said. 'It makes me think of home.'

'It's a nuisance actually because I have to fill the coke hods all the time and that means a walk across the yard several times a day in all weathers and often in the dark and I'm not convinced the dirt and fumes are good for us but you're right, it's warm and it's good for meals and baking.'

And boiling kettles, Iris thought gratefully as they sat down at the kitchen table.

'George won't eat in here,' Joyce said. 'He has to have the table set properly, it causes such a lot of work and we have to sit up in the dining room three times a day.'

'You should have help,' Iris said.

'Oh, I don't think I want any of George's parishioners in here. They already think I'm a slut and George says we can't afford to pay anybody.'

The one place in the vicarage other than the kitchen which always had a big fire was George's study. Iris was condemned to the little room next door which looked out over the back yard.

It was dusty and dark with a tiny window and the grate was black and empty. There was no evidence that a fire had been lit there in years. Iris dressed to suit after the first day but sometimes her fingers were so cold that she had difficulty in hitting the keys of her typewriter with any accuracy.

George would spend the day in his study, emerging only at mealtimes, and for church visiting, services and meetings that he had organized in the vicarage. Joyce was supposed to cater for these with sandwiches, homemade cake, tea and coffee and to have dinner parties for visiting clergy and Iris thought it was a great deal of work for someone with three children and another on the way.

The dining-room table was laid with a white cloth. Everyone had their own napkin in a silver napkin ring. The soup was tinned. The bread was white, thin and flabby. There were, however, good cakes. The 'ladies of the parish' as Joyce called them donated baking after realizing that Joyce's cakes sank in the middle or were solid so that even the birds wouldn't eat them.

Iris overheard one woman at a Mothers' Union meeting which was held at the vicarage saying to another,

'Dear Joyce is no baker and as for the state of the house and the poor little children...' and they tut-tutted together over their sponge cake with jam.

In the afternoons George would get Iris to run messages for him. Would she mind going to the post office? That didn't matter, she considered it part of her duties but when Joyce was out she was expected to attend to the door, see to visitors, make tea and coffee and the second week she was there George popped his head round the door and said, 'Mrs Robson rang and she can't clean the church. Would you mind?'

Iris looked up from the letter she was carefully typing.

'Isn't there a rota?' she said.

'Mrs Smalljohn has gone to Stanhope to visit her brother. It won't take you long.'

Iris said nothing and went but the trouble was that the church was a big place to clean, it needed sweeping, dusting, polishing. It took her several hours to bring it to a state where she would have considered it a fitting place for the congregation to spend an hour. At the end of it two women came in carrying flowers. Iris felt enthusiastic for the first time.

'Can I help?'

'Oh, no, dear,' the little fat one said, 'we don't need your help.'

'Pity you couldn't have come a couple of hours sooner,' Iris said. 'I certainly could have used yours,' and she walked out to their astonished looks.

When she got back George was in her room.

'Haven't you done those letters yet?' he said.

'No, I haven't done the letters, George, I was too busy cleaning the church.'

'It usually takes no more than a couple of hours and Iris, do you think you might call me vicar or even Mr Bell? It sounds so much better and you'd better get on with the letters. I want them in the post tonight.'

When Joyce came back Iris could hear Claire crying right along the hall and went into the kitchen to help. Joyce had been shopping and secretly to visit her mother and Wilkie since George didn't like her to go and George went off to give a talk to a local church men's society.

Iris sat Joyce down, quietened the two older children with lemonade and cake after which they went off into the playroom and Iris told Joyce about the church cleaning. Joyce sighed.

'Yes, I very often end up doing it. I suppose it's good for my soul.'

'Your soul my arse,' Iris said and they both burst out laughing. 'I would have liked doing the flowers if I'd had the chance.'

'I'm hopeless with flowers. They always look so terrible when I do them. I make a mess. They look as though I just dumped them in the vase.'

The following morning when she had done the letters and taken them into his study and was lingering there by the fire Iris ventured to George,

'I know Joyce says she doesn't want anybody here but I think she could use some proper help, don't you?'

'Joyce doesn't need any help, if she would only stir herself,' he said.

'This house is very big and you have three children,' Iris said but he was not listening, he was reading his post and frowning. 'She's pregnant, George.'

He stopped, looked at her.

'Do you know something, Iris, I remember you saying that to me once before. It's none of your business how I run my household–'

'It's an enormous place to clean–'

'Then perhaps you would like to give Joyce a hand since you are so concerned,' he said.

'You're a nasty bastard, George,' Iris said levelly and waited for him to shout and dismiss her but then she didn't care, he wasn't paying her.

To her surprise he didn't. He just went on looking at her and he said,

'There is a modern saying which goes something like "it takes one to know one". Can you look over that second letter? There's a typing error,' and he went out to do some parish visiting.

Joyce had her fourth child, another boy, soon after that and there was even more work for Iris to do.

Twenty

When people say that they had a shock and their heart stopped you know that they're talking nonsense and Iris knew, so how was it that when she thought she saw Johnny Fenwick in the street she couldn't move, she wanted to faint.

She watched as he walked down North Road on the cold wet dismal winter day in front of her. She was obliged to stop when she spotted him and as she watched his unmissable walk – it had always been one of the things she liked best about him, that he walked from the hip and easily – she forgot how to breathe.

She could not even say his name, though she opened her lips no sound came out and within moments she was telling herself not to be foolish, it could not possibly be him, she was mistaken, she was a clown but since she could not speak and her vision was no longer swimming and her legs began to move, she ran after him.

He was lost in the crowd. She looked harder. No, there he was, tall and slender, moving quickly and now he was at the end of the street and on to Framwellgate Bridge and it was starting to rain, quite suddenly, enormous drops.

The stone of the cathedral and castle was dark and the sky above them was grey and the drops were diving into the river and the rain was so heavy now that people were running from the street to get out of the downpour. The odd brave soul was putting up an umbrella in the driving rain – because once on the bridge there was no protection from the wind behind the rain – and had the added problem of seeing it blow inside out immediately.

When he was almost across, he stopped and it seemed strange to her because there was no obvious reason, nobody waiting for him, no vendor trying to sell him something. Iris, just reaching the end of the bridge beside the Coach and Eight, the pub with steps which went in a dog-leg down to the river, stopped too. She did not quite know why. The bridge was empty except for him.

The rain was coming down so hard now that the streets were deserted and she couldn't see him, he was just a dark blur. Stupidest of all, she thought, he was leaning against the top of the bridge as people did on fine days, visitors especially, marvelling at what had to be one of the most beautiful views in the world, the old houses of South Street on one side and the cathedral and castle high above the water on the other, with the fulling mill along the towpath, jutting out into the river.

The water stretched away into the distance, the greenery above the towpath providing a big floral hem which hid the lower parts of the buildings. People took photographs, gasped at the way the sun reflected off the castle windows and shimmered silver on the river but now there was nothing except him and the dark grey rain and the clouds above the small city like the day of judgement and Iris believed it must be such.

If Johnny Fenwick was alive what else could it be and she felt mad and guilty because she had wished for this, prayed for it. Had God listened to someone for the first time in history? It could not be when she was so small and insignificant. She was either crazy or dead.

Still he stood there, his tall figure bowed slightly as though he would never move again, as though the effort of the climb up Silver Street could not be faced. Oh for just five more minutes with him, Iris had thought and yet, seeing him there, she did not go forward.

She was soaked. The water was running off her hair and down her face and off her coat collar and down her neck and off the hem of her coat, off the cuffs of her coat and on to her wrists and into her boots – the bottoms of her boots were squelching.

Her thin red fingers still clutched the shopping bag and she was sure the paper bags from the greengrocers' were sodden and torn and the fruit and vegetables would be falling into the bottom of her bag, heavier as it was with water.

She waited for the rain to stop, for her vision to clear and for the ghost in front of her to disappear, as no doubt he must. She kept on trying to brush away the rain and the tears but he went on standing there so that in the end she moved, awkwardly against the heaviness of her wet clothes.

She walked very slowly and carefully across the bridge, expecting each moment that the dream would be over and she would be left with the enormous emptiness in her life, the burden she had learned so unwillingly to shoulder. She stopped just behind him and trembling, afraid, she said, hardly daring to utter his name, 'Johnny?'

There was a second and then another. He straightened. She had forgotten how tall he was and then he turned around. Iris stared into the world's most beautiful blue eyes and then the illusion shattered. It was not Johnny and his eyes were not the same, it was her expectation, her willingness that had done it.

Beneath the hat was a handsome face, eyes

almost black, the same slender cheeks and he was every inch a northern man, the Celtic dark looks that only a Border man has and he looked straight at her as Johnny had always done, but he looked blankly at her before his manners bettered his incomprehension.

'Iris,' he said, 'how are you?'

'Jack.' And all around Iris the sun came out. People magically emerged from the shops and shelters as he smiled at her.

'Would you like to go somewhere and dry off and have tea?'

Iris nodded. They went no further, only to a little cafe down the steps and to that side of the bridge. They sat by the window and the sun created a hundred thousand diamonds upon the river and the sky cleared until it was bright blue.

They had scones with thick butter and wild-strawberry jam and Earl Grey tea and Iris sat back replete and she said, 'How are your grandsons?'

'They're wonderful,' he said, 'and I care for them very much,' and then he sighed and looked out of the window at South Street, where house windows glittered in the afternoon sunshine and then he said,

'I miss my boy. Grandchildren are lovely but nothing can ever be the same as one's child.'

'I miss him too,' Iris said.

'Can I drive you home?'

She protested, she had not realized that it was late, that they had been talking for an hour. When she got home Ella was in the kitchen. Iris thought about keeping the meeting a secret but couldn't.

'Do you know who I saw?' and she told her.

'I haven't seen or heard anything about him since we got married,' Ella said. 'I suppose he doesn't spend any time here now.'

'He comes to see Johnny's children and Nan of course and he comes to Newcastle to the works.'

Iris felt like a burst balloon. She didn't understand why until later that day and the reason shocked her. She wanted to see him again.

She didn't sleep that night. She couldn't concentrate on anything.

'You seem distracted,' Ella said.

'Do I? I suppose I am, seeing Johnny's father like that.'

'You've moved on a long way since Johnny,' Ella said and Iris understood the intention behind the remark. Ella wanted her to 'move on' as she called it, as Ella had no doubt 'moved on' in her own life, or liked to think she had. Iris thought it a horrid expression, it made her sound like the contents of a house, something which could be boxed up and shifted, almost at will.

It had nothing to do with will. If it had done she would have 'moved on' a very long time ago when she had been young and had turned down his proposal of marriage. She would, she thought, have saved herself a lot of heartache and then smiled and thought, and love and fun. Regret is no use. God save me from the things that I want, I don't know what the hell I'm doing.

Was hoping that Johnny's father would get in touch 'moving on'? Iris had the feeling that it was not.

All the same, after three days of walking down to the bridge and finding nothing she was impatient and short-tempered, on the fourth day when she was there at exactly the same time as she had first seen him he was there, leaning over the bridge in the same way but not wearing a raincoat and though something told her to pretend she had not seen him and that it was only a coincidence, would mean nothing and should be ignored, she went over and leaned there beside him until he sensed her presence and turned to her.

'Isn't it beautiful?' she said.

'Miss Black. Hello.'

'Mr Fenwick.'

'I hope you don't think I'm lying in wait for you.'

'I rather hoped you were, considering that I have come here at the same time each day since we met.' Iris was appalled at her own frankness and then didn't regret it. Why should she?

He smiled.

'I couldn't get away,' he said, 'or I would have done the same.'

They went down the steps and walked along the towpath to Elvet Bridge and she loved the way that the river curved and how the cold afternoon sunshine glittered through the trees. A grey squirrel ran up a tree trunk as they passed and ducks paddled at the water's edge.

Iris could feel the happiness spread through her like good brandy, the way it had done the first time she had seen him. She had thought it was because of Johnny but this time they did not speak of his son and his company still made her glad she was there. Was it memories, she wondered.

They walked through the town and back down the steep steps of Framwellgate Bridge, up the narrow towpath and then sat in a little teashop in the old mill along the riverbank and watched the water – it was brown, from all the recent rain and was surging along like somebody important who had somewhere to go, Iris thought.

There were twigs and small branches which had no doubt been gathered from the riverbank and maybe very far up in Weardale at Wearhead or St John's Chapel or Daddry

Shield or any more of half a dozen little villages with their stone houses and little grey shops, square fields and narrow winding roads.

He was looking at her.

'What is it?' Iris said.

'Nothing. I'm so perfectly content, I'm ashamed to admit it.'

'Me too.'

'Are you?' He hesitated and then said, 'You didn't marry. Didn't you want children?'

'Doesn't everybody?'

'I'm sorry.'

'No, it was my own stupid fault. When I see Nan in the street my jealousy nearly fells me.'

He caught hold of her hand across the table and then as though he realized what he was doing let go of it almost instantly and she caught his hand back and held it for a few seconds and smiled into his eyes.

'Do you know how old I am?' he said.

'Very, very old,' she said and made him laugh.

'I am too old to sit in cafes with lovely young women.'

'So that's why you're here with me.'

'Iris—' he said and stopped.

'What?'

'Nothing. It's nice to see you, that's all.'

The tea was drunk, the plates held nothing but crumbs, the day disappeared and Iris felt obliged to say that she ought to go home and he offered to drive her there and this time she let him. His car, a Daimler, cream and luxurious, looked to Iris like a sports car with the kind of hood you could put down when the weather was fine, so that she wished it was summer now, was beautiful and when she told him this he seemed pleased.

He stopped outside the front door.

'Would you come in?' Iris said.

'Best not. Thank you.'

'When will I see you?'

He shook his head and didn't look at her.

'Why not? What harm is there in it?'

'He's dead, Iris.'

'I know but...' She stopped and then decided she had nothing to lose by saying, 'I'm so very lonely and I would like us to be friends.'

'People would gossip, even though I'm so much older, because I'm so much older. This is a very small city.'

'I won't care. Will you?'

He hesitated before he said shortly, 'Not a bit.'

'When shall we meet?'

'Very well, then. Have dinner with me.'

'Somewhere very public?'

'Yes. How about the County on Saturday night?'

'Done,' Iris said.

'I shall pick you up at half-past seven,' he

said and she agreed and got out of the car and floated into the house.

When Iris came downstairs, a little later, Ella was watching her closely. There was nobody but the two of them in the dining room. As Ella was putting mats on the table, she said, 'Whose was the gorgeous car?'

'Jack Fenwick. My mother isn't about, is she?'

'No, why?'

'I'm having dinner with him on Saturday evening, at the County, and I don't think she would approve.'

'Oh,' Ella said again and with awful timing, David arrived back from work at that moment and said,

'Having dinner with?'

'Jack Fenwick,' Ella supplied when Iris didn't answer.

'Johnny's father?' He looked surprised.

'Yes,' Iris said.

'Well, that's nice,' he said and she was then surprised.

'You don't think I shouldn't?'

'Why ever not? You'll have lots to talk about. Where did you meet him?'

'In town, the other day.'

'Good,' he said and disappeared.

When they went to bed that night Ella turned from brushing her hair at the dressing table and said to her husband, 'Do you really think it's wise for Iris to be seen with Jack Fenwick?'

David frowned. 'Why shouldn't she?'

'What if people get the wrong idea?'

'What wrong idea?'

'Don't be so dense, David! It's like one of us going around with somebody sixteen.'

He laughed.

'I don't think it is. They probably have nothing to gain but memories of Johnny which no doubt is all they talk about and anyway...'

'And anyway what?'

'I don't see what difference it makes. Jack Fenwick is a very warm man.'

'That has nothing to do with it. He's far too old for her,' she said.

David laughed harder.

'What if he hurts her?' Ella insisted.

'She's an adult. What do you want me to do, tell her to stay at home? She must be bored witless by now.'

'I didn't even know you noticed.'

He looked uncomfortable and began undressing, turned sideways so that she couldn't see his expression, she thought.

'Of course I noticed. She's my sister. Egypt broke her heart.'

'Johnny dying?'

'That and the rest. She's never really come out of it. It was all so bloody awful. If going

266

out to dinner with Jack Fenwick makes any difference then why shouldn't she?'

'And when people gossip?'

'Oh, to hell with other people,' he said, and stripped off his tie.

Twenty-One

Iris was excited right from the beginning about having dinner at the County with Jack Fenwick. She never did such things. Ella, having seemed disapproving, said, when there was a lull after breakfast the next morning, 'Whatever will you wear?'

'What?' Iris was taken aback. The kitchen, thankfully, was empty.

'On Saturday evening. You can't go in just anything you know.'

Iris's faint irritation was overcome by the idea that her sister-in-law was sufficiently enthusiastic to offer help.

'Would you like to borrow something of mine?' Ella offered.

Iris would really have liked a new dress but there was not much time and also Ella had dresses that more discerning women than she would have sacrificed months of their lives to wear.

Ella held on her face the impish expression which Iris had grown to love and reminded her that if she had had a sister it would have been like this.

They went upstairs and found the perfect dress for Iris, pale-grey silk, with little tucks

in the bodice, tight-fitting, with a low neck-
line and full-length skirt which swished
when she moved. As she turned around,
looking at herself in the mirror Ella said,

'You look divine.'

'Nonsense.'

'Yes, you do. My God, Iris, you look good.'

Feeling almost as good as Ella said she
looked Iris beamed at her. Iris felt obliged to
tell her mother. Lottie shook her head but
she didn't say anything.

It was, Iris thought, a proper dinner, soup,
fish, meat, pudding and cheese, but she
would not have noticed if they had been
eating cardboard. There was, she knew, no
place here for women alone and no reason
for them to be there, neither was it the kind
of place where women would have gone in
pairs if they had nobody but a friend to go
with.

Everybody was a couple, there was no help
for it. She had to keep reminding herself
that she was part of a couple. It was difficult
not to be smug. Jack Fenwick was obviously
well known. The staff said, 'Good evening,
Mr Fenwick,' and gave him the best table. It
looked out across the river.

Iris gazed at the water and the lights of the
houses on Claypath bank across at the other
side because some of them were three-
storeyed and lit the movement of the water

as it busily flowed on its way to Sunderland and the river mouth.

'Oh, it's perfect,' she said.

They had had white wine to go with the sole and red wine to go with the beef and dessert wine for the pudding and the cheese but she was very careful not to drink too much. She was not used to a lot of alcohol and she was no longer a girl, taking her drink easily. She didn't want to do or say the wrong thing.

She declined brandy and was glad because so did he but they sat in the quietness of the lounge where a huge log fire burned, and they drank their coffee.

'Are you all right?' he asked, a trifle anxiously, Iris thought.

'I'm very happy. Don't I look it?'

'You look beautiful.'

'It's Ella's dress,' Iris said in confusion. 'Thank goodness we're the same size.'

Other people were having coffee and she had noticed all through the evening, people looking across but she did not want to see anybody she knew, she did not want anybody to intrude upon this private idyll. So it was unfortunate that one of her father's friends approached the low table where they were sitting and said with an avid stare,

'Good evening, Miss Black. Good evening, Fenwick.'

'Mr Forbes. How are you?' Iris responded

faintly. She could not hide her disappointment. Could she not have one perfect evening without somebody thinking it could be improved by his presence?

Jack merely smiled and nodded.

'Perhaps you would like to join my wife and myself?' the man said. 'We haven't seen you in so long, Iris. How unusual to find you here and in such ... such elevated company.' He looked towards Jack and Iris turned once again to look out of the window.

'Another time, perhaps,' Jack said smoothly.

'Oh, but I insist.'

Jack didn't say anything else. He shook his head slightly and he also looked out of the window. The other man blustered a few words which Iris did not hear and then he went away. Safe now, Iris looked at Jack.

'I'm not sure that was terribly polite,' she said.

'He certainly wasn't. Curious people.'

'I meant you.'

He met her eyes, acknowledged the remark with a grin.

'Well, you were a big help,' he said.

'What was I supposed to say?' Iris said and couldn't help but giggle. 'He'll think we're terribly rude.'

'When you're rich,' he said, 'rudeness is expected.'

The way that he said it, as if against

himself and lightly, made Iris laugh.

'Are you so very rich?'

'My dear girl, you have no idea,' he said.

The days went by and he did not contact her. After a full week Iris was so agitated that Ella noticed.

'Is something wrong?' she said, mid-evening, when David had gone off to a Masonic dinner, the children were in bed and the house was quiet.

Iris considered saying no and that she was having an early night but somehow she wanted to tell somebody how very unhappy she was.

'Jack Fenwick hasn't been in touch since we had dinner,' she said.

'Did you expect him to?'

Iris looked at her.

'What do you mean?'

'Even you must have run out of conversation about Johnny by now.'

'It isn't like that, Ella.'

'No?'

Iris was almost ashamed.

'I like him,' she said.

'I see.'

Iris stole another look at her.

'Maybe we should have a drink,' Ella said.

Nobody spoke until they had sat down and were both smoking a cigarette and had glasses of Scotch in their hands. Iris rarely smoked but tonight the alcohol and nicotine were bliss.

'Perhaps he doesn't like to,' Ella said.

'What do you mean?'

'He's a lot older than you and you loved his son. That's a very complicated thing for any man to face.'

'You don't think he just didn't fancy me?' Iris said and to her ears the simple local term sounded so apt.

'He would have to be made of concrete not to fancy you,' Ella said.

Iris laughed but was grateful and so pleased to think that Ella would say such things just to make her feel good about herself.

'I have the feeling he's...'

'What?'

'Rich men attract women.'

'He's not married.'

'Maybe he doesn't need to.'

'Maybe he hadn't met the right woman until he saw you.'

Iris could have hugged her.

'What can I do?'

'Well,' Ella took a slug of her Scotch, 'you have several options. You can assume that he doesn't want to see you again and settle for that, or you could think that he thinks the situation is too delicate and therefore isn't seeing you again or you can wait for him to ring...' She hesitated.

'Or?' Iris prompted, surmising there was more.

'Or you could telephone him, or ... if it were me I'd go and see him.'

'Oh, Ella, I don't think I could.'

'What do you have to lose?'

'It would be so humiliating if he didn't want to see me again.'

'People don't die of humiliation,' Ella said briskly.

After that Iris played games in her mind. She wouldn't go and see him because he didn't want her. He was probably away on business and from what she could discover he was rarely at home so it would be a wasted journey. She would wait, he could ring.

Nothing happened. She visited the bridge where they had met. After another week she was frustrated, angry. After a further day she had made up her mind that he didn't care. Two days on she was in tears and wished him dead and put him from her mind. An hour after that she had borrowed Ella's little green car and was out of the city.

She didn't give herself time to think, she just drove, through the little pit villages which lay beyond the city and then into Rowarth where the castle lay.

She hated it. She had always hated the tumbledown little village with the one-storeyed stone cottages at either side of the road which no doubt at one time had housed the people who worked at his blasted castle.

The huge gates were open. She swept along the narrow drive until the castle came into view and it was only then that the enormity of what she had done came upon her and she stopped the car and gazed through the rain which was falling fast and she regarded the dark walls of the castle where last she had been with Johnny so many years ago and she sat in the gathering gloom, wanting to cry.

Why wasn't he there? Why had things changed so much? Why wouldn't it ever be as you wanted it to be and who in hell's name was the stupid bloody woman who had turned down the man she loved when he proposed to her so long ago?

She battered the steering wheel with both hands, thinking as she did so, sorry Ella, but the little car was solid and withstood the assault.

I know why I turned him down. Marriage. Who in hell invented such a stupid thing and why oh why do people go on conforming to it?

She breathed carefully for a few moments and then got out of the car, slammed the door and trudged towards the enormous building, across the grass which was the most direct route.

The grass was long, thick, wet and slippery. She could see a door up a huge flight of outside steps. The banister on them soaked her glove as she put a hand on it for assistance and then she trod up the uneven steps and hammered on the big oak door.

She did this twice before the door opened and a young woman stood there.

Iris tried to smile and couldn't.

'Is Mr Fenwick at home? I should like to see him. I'm Iris Black.'

'Oh, do come in,' the woman said, 'it's not fit to be outside.'

Iris went thankfully into a huge hall. Her heart beat fast. She gazed around her. It was vast, stretched so far upwards that she had to crane her neck. She didn't remember it being this large. Maybe things got bigger as you got older or had she been so much in love that she hadn't noticed?

The woman led her unceremoniously to double doors and opened them and said,

'Mr Fenwick, Miss Black is here.'

Iris stepped inside. It was the biggest room that she had ever seen and in it two huge log fires burned and it was a library, lined with books. There were two definite areas, one was like a study with a huge leather-topped square desk and the other contained armchairs grouped around the fire.

Jack Fenwick got up from where he had been sitting at the desk and he looked at her in some surprise. Iris was inclined to apologize or say something rude and when she could manage neither she just stood, feeling even smaller than usual, the room somehow getting bigger and bigger around her.

'Why, Iris,' he said. 'Would you like some tea?'

Iris found her voice but her throat blocked up and she was acutely aware of how close she was to losing control of her emotions

'Don't be idiotic,' she said. 'Do you think I've come here to play tea parties? You didn't ring me or – or anything.'

'I couldn't.'

'Why not? Surely in this bloody ghastly heap of a place you have a telephone?' and she smiled through the fog of her now-dimmed eyes in his general direction. 'Even if you never wanted to see me again it would have been good manners.'

'I don't have any manners left,' he said.

Nobody spoke, and in the silence, which reached way up into the far-off ceiling of the room, the logs fell apart in the grate and the sound of the rain on the windows was heavy and thick and echoed in the room over and over.

Iris wanted to run. She felt as though she had committed some huge faux pas, made a mistake she could not retrieve anything from. Jack Fenwick did not want her. He did not want her in his house, he had not wanted her in his life and she had broken every rule of society by coming here to him when he had not asked her.

She thought back to the dancing when she had been very young and how you had to wait for a boy to ask you, you couldn't go to them, it wasn't acceptable. It was like being an object, you were forward if you did the asking, you were too keen, cheap, were indicating that you could be used like a whore. It was, she acknowledged now, one of the worst ideas that a male-dominated society had produced and he was making use of it now, at least she thought he was.

'There you were,' she said, 'safe in your ivory tower and here I am, intruding.'

'Iris–'

'You could at least have let me know.'

'It wasn't that.'

'What was it, then?' Suddenly she was unafraid of the brilliant intellect which he so obviously chose not to display to anyone, the vast wealth which he could not hide, the cold exclusiveness which came from such things. She had nothing but her dignity left to lose and she no longer cared about that.

'Come on, Jack, tell me what it was.' Her voice echoed across the vast room. 'Have you become so very important that you can treat me or any woman like this? Who do you think you are?'

'It wasn't that,' he said again.

'You're like a stuck record,' she said.

'Don't bully me, Iris.'

'Why not? What are you going to do, have me thrown out of this dreadful pile? Just tell me why I'm not allowed to see you. Is that what you do, you think you can discard women like holey socks?'

It made him smile a little, the image she evoked.

'I never thought of you like a holey sock,' he said, 'and I don't think I discarded you.'

'How did you think of me?'

'I thought of you in my son's arms,' he said.

For some reason it was the very last thing she would ever have expected him to say and because of it Iris felt she could have cried the Wear. She shook her head as though she could disperse his words that way.

'I loved him,' she said.

'No, I don't think you did.'

Iris stared across the enormous space between them.

'Why should you say a thing like that to me?'

'Because it's true.' He looked at her for the first time in minutes. 'You would have married him if you had loved him.'

'Why do men always think women want to marry them?'

'Because when you love someone you want to be with them, the only thing in your whole universe is to have them come home to you and the most wonderful thing in the world is to allow yourself the huge risk of committing yourself to someone and knowing that you are safe because they love you. It's astonishing and when it happens you've had everything. It cheats death because it is the entire purpose of life, the height of our very existence. Once you've loved and been loved like that nothing matters. Nan loved Johnny like that, but he loved you–'

'I won't take the blame for this,' Iris said.

'Why not? It's partly yours.'

'Partly? And who does the rest belong to?'

'Me.'

'Why you?' Iris tried to laugh but it stuck in her throat like a too large boiled sweet.

'Because you didn't love Johnny after you saw me.'

Iris couldn't move and it took some time for her to manage, amidst rising panic, to say, 'Why you conceited, arrogant, old bastard!'

'He was just a boy. He was my son and I loved him but you ... you fell in love with me the minute you saw me. You had just got out of his bed and you thought you loved him and then...'

He didn't go on. The panic rose in Iris's stomach and in her throat and prevented speech.

'You didn't marry him because we had

breakfast together,' Jack said. 'It was as simple as that. Life makes fools of us all. Please go now.'

Something made Iris not move.

'And you?' she said.

'I loved you from the moment I saw you standing there in the sunlight.'

'It isn't true,' was all Iris could manage and then she turned and ran out of the building and down to the car, her breath coming in such strange bursts that she could hardly move. She didn't cry, she started up the little car and tore down to the road until she reached the castle gates and then she started to lose control of herself. She didn't pull into the road, she sat there and sobbed until she thought she would never stop.

Twenty-Two

George was the last person Iris wanted to see late one evening when the winter had released its hold and the days were beginning to lengthen and it was warm. She was trying to learn to live without Jack Fenwick, as she had learned to live without his son, she told herself. Why on earth would George want to see her and when she had more important things on her mind?

'Sour-faced he is too,' Flo said. She had let him in.

The sitting room being full of people, Iris opted for the cool of the garden and sat George down on a wrought-iron bench which had stood for years under the porch window. It was a lovely place to sit of an evening and had she been alone Iris would have been happier there.

'Is everything all right, George?' Iris said when he declined to speak.

'This is all your fault, Iris.'

'What is?' Iris said, looking keenly at him.

George fidgeted for a few moments while Iris tried to admire the view beyond the bottom of the garden and when she had waited and waited she said,

'For goodness' sake, George, just spit it out!'

He glared at her.

'I thought Joyce might be here. Failing that, I thought you might have gone on holiday with her and the children.'

'Have you been at the pop?'

Her flippancy was too much for him. George jumped to his feet.

'She's gone away,' he said, gazing away down the garden.

'Do you mean she's left you?'

'She hasn't left me. I mean ... I like to think not. I like to think...'

'It doesn't surprise me,' Iris said.

George had to turn to glare at her this time but somehow he managed it.

'You did it,' he said. 'I should never have let you come to the house, you were always a bad influence. It seemed like a good idea at the time.'

'Have you been to Wilkie's?'

'I wouldn't set foot there.'

'Why not?' When he didn't reply Iris said, 'People can't help being poor, you know. Greedy governments, greedy capitalists make it so.'

'What are you, Iris, a socialist?'

'Do you know, I think I am? It would be wonderful if the poor and disadvantaged were given opportunities instead of being exploited.' She glanced towards the sitting-room windows, wondering if her brother could hear. 'This place should be one of the richest on earth, all the industry, all the resources, instead it's full of grubby little pit villages and people who have nothing because it was all taken away from them by unscrupulous owners. The Church of course was always a big owner.'

'Don't bring politics into this. I want my wife back.'

'In that case I suggest you go to your sister-in-law's.'

'You don't know she's there.'

'Where else could she be with a baby and three children? With no money and no help she could hardly take to the open road or hole up in an expensive hotel.' Iris stood up, she wanted to go to Heath Houses and make sure Joyce was safe and if George wasn't prepared to go with her she would ask Ella for the loan of her car and go right now.

'I never wanted to marry her,' George said.

'I know you didn't.'

'You told her to, didn't you?' He shot her a direct look.

'Me?'

'Yes.'

'What else could she do?'

George looked confused.

'I don't believe that Matthew is mine,' he

said, his voice flat with hurt.

He gazed across the garden, past the lawns to the big trees at the bottom where David and his friends had played when they were small children. Iris had always liked those trees because of that, it all had something to do with the going-on of families.

'Do you think Joyce was promiscuous?' she said, making her voice sound shocked.

'No. I don't think that. I think, like an awful lot of people, she made mistakes.'

'And you didn't?'

'Of course I did. My marriage is evidence of it. I didn't love her and I knew she didn't love me.'

'You have four beautiful children. There are much worse things.'

'It was you I wanted,' George said.

Iris was silenced. George walked a few steps away from her and embarrassment. He walked down the crazy-paving path and though the roses were not yet in bloom he stood and gazed at them as if they were. Iris wondered where Jack was and what he was doing and her heart gave a horrible little twist.

'We planted cabbages among the roses during the war,' she said.

George looked at her then.

'You were something I aspired to, your way of life was something I would have cared for very much. You seemed to have everything. I'm just a farm boy from a rural village who did better than the rest. My mother wanted me not to be a farm labourer.'

'Do you know I had no idea,' Iris said. 'I always thought you were so desperately middle class.' She couldn't remember his mother at all from the wedding.

'I didn't have to get this far, a job in a shop would have pleased her.'

'She must be very proud of you.'

'She's dead. She was so ashamed when I had to marry Joyce. Joyce's family were common.'

This aspect of the situation had not occurred to Iris and gave her a few guilty moments among all the others she had.

'They were very good respectable people,' she said, 'and still are and if you treated her better things might improve.'

George laughed.

'You think so?'

'What else is there?'

'I hate being at home,' George said.

'Don't you love your children?'

'I don't think I like children, they take all her time, all her attention. We've never had any time to ourselves, to discover whether we might have liked one another. It's too late now. We're trapped, like so many people.'

'I'm going to Heath Houses. Will you

come with me?'

He didn't answer.

Iris went inside. Her brother and Ella were in the sitting room, listening to some music. Clyde was playing on the floor, Susan was asleep on the rug. Why couldn't Joyce and George be like that, Iris wondered and then her conscience told her that David had not been manoeuvred into marrying Ella, he had married her because he wanted to and that was why it worked.

She told them that she thought Joyce was at Heath Houses, that George had decided not to go.

'May I borrow your car, Ella?'

'I'll come with you,' David said. 'You can't bring them all back, Ella's car is too small.'

She felt so grateful to him that she smiled.

'You don't know I'm bringing them back.'

'Surely they have to, it isn't practical for them to stay there.'

It was easier to let somebody else drive. She presumed George had gone back to his vicarage. There was no sign of him. She directed David into the front street.

'Shall I stay here?' he offered, halting the car.

'You don't mind?' Iris was grateful for the thousandth time for her brother's sensitivity. 'Only if there is a problem, I think she'll talk more freely if there's just me.'

'Go on,' David said and leaned across and

opened the door for her.

Iris went across the road. It was quite late now. She could see lights ahead. She banged on the door and after a short time when somebody peeped through the curtains and she thought she could hear conversation the door opened just a tiny bit.

'Wilkie, it's me, Iris.'

'Oh.' The sound of relief. The door opened wide. 'Come in. Who's that with you in the car? It isn't George?'

'It's David. He isn't coming in but he wanted to help.'

'Tell him to come in.' Her voice was soft.

'Are you sure?'

'You can talk to Joyce by yourself if you like but it would be nicer if he came in,' Wilkie said.

Joyce had not just decided to leave George, the problem had got bigger and bigger in her mind. She had kept telling herself that he did not treat her badly but the truth was that he had always done so and it was her own fault, she had to acknowledge it now because she had treated him badly when she married him, though what on earth else she could have done she could never think.

George had acted like the wounded party for so long that it had become part of their marriage. She accepted that they did not like one another though George would conveniently forget this at bedtime and was always reaching for her.

After four children Joyce had decided that she did not want George reaching out for her in the darkness. She did not tell him this, she just had a headache, heard one of the children crying, could not sleep and would stay downstairs to read or had stomach ache and would go into the spare room, cool as it was even in summer if the day had been wet. In the spare room, which had in it a double bed, Joyce would think of what it would be like having a double bed all to yourself all the time and not having George there. The idea became more and more appealing and so did her excuses at bedtime.

'You cannot have a headache again,' he complained after a week.

'I don't want any more children.'

All this, as they undressed for bed. Finally she had been able to say something of the truth. It was not in fact the truth. The children were not the problem, it was George's desires, George's needs which had turned more and more into disgusting needs somehow as they had gone along and she knew really that they would not have been disgusting if she and George could have agreed better outside of the bedroom, if George had just sometimes been kind.

'You don't like me,' she said, made braver by her first words. 'I don't want to sleep with you any more.'

George laughed but it was not that he thought her funny, it was the idea that she should say, even think such things.

'Don't be ridiculous,' he said, 'we're married.'

Joyce put on her nightdress and tried to get out of the room and looking back she thought that was when her patience ended because she tried to get out and George tried to stop her. He pushed the door shut but left his hand on it and that hand frightened her and so did the way that he looked at her.

'Where do you think you're going?' he said and his voice frightened her too.

'I'm going to sleep in the spare room.'

'Oh, no, you're not,' he said.

'I can go if I want.'

'No, you can't.'

She went to the door, she tried to open it and George pushed her. He didn't hit her, he didn't knock her over, it was nothing dramatic like that but he pushed her towards the bed and her heart beat hard.

'You're my wife. You'll sleep with me.'

She began to cry, she tried to get near the door again, she got up and George pushed her again. That was all it was. After that he told her to get into bed and she did and then he got in and they turned their backs on one another.

They didn't sleep. She hoped that one of the children would cry but the silence in the night went on and on and she lay there, eyes wide open, and wished and wished that the morning would come.

When it did they behaved just as they always did and she was amazed that George thought she would accept what he had said and what he had done. At the first opportunity she gathered the children around her and left. She took nothing with her, otherwise she knew she would not have been able to go, not allowed. She would not spend another night there.

Up narrow dark stairs and into a tiny bedroom, Iris found Joyce sitting on the bed, surrounded by children. Matthew, the eldest, had grown so much she thought he was almost an adult and he came and stood defensively in front of his mother.

'It's just me, Matt,' Iris said.

'She isn't going back there to be treated like a skivvy,' Matthew said.

Joyce put a hand on her son's arm and after a moment or two he left the room. Iris listened to him clattering down the stairs. The little girl was asleep, Wilkie had taken the baby. The other boy sat close beside his mother.

'George came to see me,' Iris said.

'He didn't bother himself to come here,'

Joyce said.

'He's worried about you.'

'So worried that he wouldn't come after me. He only wants me there because his bishop says man and wife should always be together. He doesn't want me and I can't stand it any more, Iris, I can't. I'm not going back because of the Church or for George.'

She began to cry.

'What has he done?' Iris said, looking at the boy but finding it impossible to ask this obscurely.

'Nothing. Nothing anybody could point to and say was his fault. He doesn't hit me. He shouts but not when the children are there. He drinks a bit too much. We don't have any money of course but that's because of his job. He doesn't like me. He never liked me and I never liked him.'

'I wish I hadn't persuaded you to marry him,' Iris said.

'Oh, don't feel guilty for something I did. We were making the best of a bad job. I was in love with Melvyn.' She laughed shortly, bitterly. 'Can you imagine? I just want to stay here with Wilkie and my mother now.'

'But, Joyce, how can you? Wilkie can barely afford to keep herself and her mother in this tiny house. How on earth could she keep you all?'

'I don't know but I cannot go back to that life. I never stop cleaning and cooking and

292

seeing to the children. I have no friends but you. I'm not going back, I don't care what you say or George does.'

The little sitting room was so dark, David didn't think he had ever been in such an ill-lit room before and it was tiny, only space for a sofa and one chair and there were himself, the boy, Wilkie and her mother in it. Wilkie offered to make tea. David accepted.

'I'm so glad you came, Mr Black.'

David smiled at her.

'Why don't you ever call me David?' he said. 'I call you Wilkie. I always think of you as Iris's best friend.'

'I try to be.'

'You are very important to her and to all of us,' he said. Wilkie smiled brilliantly at him and there was passion in her dark eyes.

'Do you know I think I knew your father?' Wilkie's mother said.

'Did you?' David was glad to talk to anybody about his father, he missed him so much.

'You look very like him. He was a wonderful man. Not like other men in his position. He cared about people. I dare say you're the same.'

'I don't know,' David said, in some confusion.

'You must be,' Bess said, 'that's why you're here, because you thought you could help.'

'I would like to,' David said.

'I wish Joyce had never married George,' Bess said as the boy snuggled down beside her in her chair. 'There was no way round it, no other choice for a woman in her position. She made a good nurse when she helped out at the hospital during the war, it was a shame. George is mean-spirited, that's his trouble. Isn't it funny, clergymen are supposed to be good to people and guide them and set an example? Most of them don't know the first thing about the hard lives people lead and have no idea how to help.'

'My mother wanted me to go into the Church,' David said. 'I couldn't have, of course, my father needed the help in the foundry but I would have liked to go into the navy.'

He didn't understand why he was saying all this, just that Wilkie's mother was the kind of woman who inspired you to talk to her.

'Did she really?' Bess looked closely at him. 'Do you know I think she might have had the right of it?'

'Tea, David?' Wilkie gave him a flowered cup and saucer.

'Thank you, Wilkie.'

'David is a lovely name,' Bess said.

It is a lovely name, Wilkie thought.

Iris plodded down the stairs.

'She isn't going anywhere, at least not tonight,' she said.

'We can come back in the morning,' David said. 'Things might look better then.'

'We cannot manage and that's the truth of it. I could go out to work but Joyce cannot manage four bairns, the shop and my mother,' Wilkie said.

'Would you like me to go and talk to George?' David offered. 'He should at least be allowed to know where his children are.'

Wilkie hesitated and then nodded. Iris kissed Wilkie's warm cheek and then they left. When they were safely in the car David said,

'He has to come and get his wife and children, there's no other way round this.'

'We must find a better solution.'

'Can you think of one?'

'Not offhand,' Iris said and she sighed.

David dropped her off at home. Iris was so glad to have a home, so grateful not to be living in a little hovel, pleased to be out of the problem, at least for the time being, relieved that David had offered to handle part of it. She was tired now, she felt guilty, responsible, wished things different.

'She had no right to walk out like that,' George said, 'no right at all.'

The vicarage was, David thought, one of the most dismal houses he had ever been inside. The echoing rooms went on forever and it seemed enormous with just George in it. There was even a sweeping staircase which led off into the darkness. It was enough to make anybody shudder.

It was cold, it had tiny fireplaces which would not have kept a cupboard warm. It smelled of a kind of poverty which had none of the cosiness of the little house he had just left and David knew what it was, it was lack of affection, there was no harmony here.

'I'm her husband. You should have brought her back.'

'She didn't want to come back. Maybe tomorrow you should go there and talk to her.'

'I will do nothing of the sort,' George said. 'She chose to leave. She ... she doesn't know any of the things you would expect your wife to know. She's ill-read, ill-informed. She was always beneath me.'

George, David surmised, must have been on the communion wine or sherry to talk like this. He just wished he didn't have to hear it.

'She has four children, man, go there and get her. You have a lot of room here and the pit cottage is so small and your children are confused and upset. Couldn't you offer her family a home?'

'You've met her sister. She's a dreadful woman, big and bossy, the kind of woman men can't stand and her mother is one of those old pit wives.'

'They have nothing,' David said. 'Their father is dead. You're the only man in the family.' He wanted to awaken some kind of paternal instinct in George but he wasn't hopeful.

'Why don't you have them at your house if you're so keen?' was all George said.

David left. He didn't know what else to say or do. He could not believe that George would go on letting three women and his four children live in a tiny house in a pit row with very little money when he had half a dozen bedrooms, four huge reception rooms and a garden which would have fed a street if it were planted with vegetables.

When he got home Iris and Ella were in the sitting room. His mother had gone to bed.

'What did he say?' Iris said, running into the hall, closely followed by Ella.

'Nothing very coherent. I think he'd been at the cocktail cabinet,' David said, 'which is exactly where I'd like to be. Would somebody pour me a stiff Scotch?'

Ella hurried back into the dining room to do so. Iris looked at him.

'What are we to do?'

'We could offer them to come here. That was what George said.'

'The bastard,' Iris said but she kept her

voice down because her mother was upstairs. Then she looked at him as though she
had never seen him before and she did
something she hadn't done in a long time.
She kissed him.

'You're a good man, David,' she said,
'there aren't many like you.'

Ella had poured drinks for them all and
smiled as she pushed a glass at Iris. They
went into the living room and sat down.

Iris took a big gulp of her Scotch before
she said, 'I'm going to go back to nursing.'

'I thought you didn't want to,' Ella
protested.

'Somebody has to keep Joyce and the
children and I could rent a house for us all.'

Nobody said anything. David looked at his
wife and then at his sister.

'That's very noble,' he said, 'but it isn't a
good idea.'

'Neither is having them to live here what
with all of us,' Iris said. 'It isn't fair on you
and Ella and ... it just wouldn't work.'

Twenty-Three

Iris did not really know what she could accomplish by going to see George but she went anyway. George, having seen her arrive, came out of his study. He was unshaven and looked to her experienced eyes like a man who had had several drinks.

'What do you want?' he said.

'I still work for you, at least officially, don't I?'

'You have no compunction, have you, Iris, no better feelings,' George said.

'Is Joyce here?'

'Of course she's not here. She's still with her dreadful sister.'

'You should speak more respectfully of women who nursed during the war,' Iris said. 'She saved many a better neck than yours.'

'Why don't you get out of here, Iris, and don't come back,' George said and he went into his study and slammed the door.

'I feel as if this is all my fault,' Iris told Wilkie the following day.

They were standing outside in the back lane.

'Joyce did this herself,' Wilkie said. She stopped here and glanced up and down the lane but nobody was hanging out their washing, it not being a Monday, or sitting in their yards, it not being a bright day, or leaning over the back gate, gossiping. 'We tried to make it better.'

'We made it worse.'

'There was no alternative.'

'George is claiming Matthew isn't his.'

'We may become glad in the future if he isn't,' Wilkie said. 'The next thing is to get the children into school, that'll take care of them except weekends, evenings and holidays. I shall do what I wanted to do when I first came back and go into nursing. Joyce will have to manage the shop, Mother, the house and feeding and looking after us all.'

She saw the look Iris could not hide and said, 'There's no other way.'

'I'll come over and help Joyce in the house and with the children.'

'Iris,' Wilkie looked squarely at her, 'this is not your problem.'

'I've got nothing else to do. Please let me help.'

'You can take the car,' Ella suggested as Iris was about to leave. It was a week later. Iris looked gratefully at her.

'I can get the bus.'

'You've been getting the bus every day.

I've got a few things for you.'

A few things was two big bags of groceries, a pile of games which had been Iris and David's which Lottie had discovered in the attic and at least a dozen books. There were also magazines, some sweets and various clothes.

'Wilkie will be so pleased with this lot,' Iris said.

It was Lottie's birthday. David, Ella, Iris and Lottie were attending a dinner dance at the Waterloo Hotel in Elvet, a part of Durham to the side where Swan Island had been and which held the law courts, the prison, colleges for the university and went on to the green fields at the south of the little city where the road went on towards Darlington.

Lottie had requested the dinner and David had thought it a nice idea that there was a band, music, his mother had always loved dancing and now that his father was not there she did not have many chances to do so.

'I'm going to dance her off her feet,' he told Iris.

It was pleasant being there, all dressed up, eating a good dinner, drinking claret and listening to the music and the sound of people talking and Iris was happy until she saw the tall dark well-dressed man come in with several other people and her mood hit the carpet.

'What is it?' David asked, following her gaze as his mother and Ella chatted at the far side of the table.

'Nothing.'

'Jack Fenwick.'

'Oh my God, he's seen us,' Iris said, suppressing a desire to hide under the table.

Jack Fenwick said something to the spectacular blonde woman who was with him, gazed across the room and then came over. Iris had to stop herself from running out of the room. All Jack said was good evening. Iris looked at anything but him. She did not even hear what he was saying, as though she was blocking her ears with her fists.

He did not linger. Iris could not look at him though she was sure she gazed dimly out from her corner beside the wall. When he had asked them how they were and they had returned the compliment he went back to his dining companions. Iris escaped to the ladies' room only to find that Ella followed her.

'Are you all right?' she said.

'I was until that bastard arrived,' was all Iris could manage. Ella glanced around but there was nobody else in the room and then as Iris began to cry she said,

'What has he done?'

'He thinks I'm in love with him,' Iris said, feeling stupid even as she said it. What other explanation could she give?

Instead of being rude or discounting the remark her sister-in-law looked levelly at her and said, 'And are you?'

'He told me I hadn't married Johnny because of him and it isn't true.'

'Then why are you so upset?'

'Because it's partly true,' Iris admitted as she sat down on a stool in front of the mirror and she found a handkerchief in her bag and rubbed it across her face, regardless of the mess it was no doubt doing to her make-up.

Ella sat down on the stool at the next mirror.

'You love him?'

'I do, yes. Isn't it awful?'

'And does he love you?'

Iris's handkerchief smelled of what her mother called 'Midnight at Woollies' and was not big enough for anybody to cry into.

'He said he had loved me since the moment we met.'

'I see.'

Iris glared at Ella's pretty face, her pearl earrings, her pearl necklace, her dark eyes.

'No, you don't see. He's ... he's far too old and...' Somehow she felt old these days whereas Jack didn't seem any older than the day they had met, in fact he seemed younger, that was the silly part of growing older yourself. After a while some people met in the middle. 'Johnny is ...I feel guilty and I think he ... because of his son.'

'But you didn't do anything about it at the time?'

'I didn't even realize, at least ... I didn't want to because ... it was such a betrayal on both our parts. Johnny is dead and I cared about him and...'

'But Jack is here.'

Iris got to her feet. She couldn't sit there any longer.

'He doesn't want me. He told me he didn't want to see me.'

Ella sighed and then turned and looked at her flawless complexion.

'Well, this is your mother's evening and we haven't had any pudding yet so I suggest we go back into the dining room if you can't think of anything else,' she said.

'Quite right,' Iris said, blowing her nose as best she could and then repairing her lipstick.

They went back and sat down again. Her mother looked concerned, her brow was furrowed. Iris kissed her at her enquiry.

'They are bringing the dessert menu and I'm going to order coffee,' David said. 'You did want coffee, Iris?'

When she next could not help looking up, Jack Fenwick was seated with his back to her. Iris ached for him, physically, mentally. If there had been other ways in which she could have done so she felt she would have. She watched the blonde woman, who was laughing and talking to him. Iris had to make herself order sherry trifle when the dessert menu arrived.

Iris didn't understand what she was doing except that she waited until the house was quiet and then stole downstairs and took Ella's car keys and within minutes was pushing the accelerator on the little car so that it stotted.

She didn't stop to think until she turned in at the open gates of the castle. All was quiet but there were lights on. For a few moments she considered whether Jack might have brought the blonde woman back with him or whether in fact he might have people staying, which seemed reasonable. What if she was there, what if everybody who had been with him was staying at the castle, but no, as she reached the building lights burned in only one area so it seemed unlikely.

She considered knocking and then turned the big iron circle which opened the door at the top of the steps and it gave. In the hall it was dark but a door was ajar so she made her way along the vast wide hall, trying to stay in the middle of the carpet so that the sound of her heels would not clip-clop as she walked. She reached the door, listening, but the only sound that she could discern was the crackling of a fire. She pushed at the heavy door. Jack was sitting to one side of the fire with a glass in his hand.

'Hello, Iris,' he said.

Iris stood in the doorway.

'You were expecting me,' she said.

'That would have been presumptuous.'

'Do you have people staying?'

'No.'

'Not even the ... the glamorous blonde?'

Jack considered his drink.

'The glamorous blonde, alas, is not mine,' he said. 'Do come in. Would you like a drink?'

'I just ... it's been such a long time,' Iris said.

He poured Scotch for her, handed it to her.

'How's Nan? Do the boys go away to school?'

'I see them a lot when I'm in London. Nan's mother died.'

'She must be lonely.'

'She gave up the house here. She too lives in London, not too far away from me. She sees the boys most weekends.'

'That must be nice,' Iris said. 'Jack...'

'Oh, please, don't say Jack that way. We were managing the small talk so beautifully. Tell me about your life. Sit down. What are you doing these days?'

She sat down and took a slug of Scotch

and told him about George and Joyce and Wilkie and her mother.

'I feel so responsible,' she said.

'I can't think why you should. George, like other men, must learn to pay for his mistakes.'

'But such a small mistake.'

'Perhaps in comparison to some.'

'Jack–'

He said, 'Iris–' at the same time and they both stopped.

The sound of the fire which was big and bright with logs, was suddenly noisy, roaring up the chimney and broke the silence between them. Iris was glad of it but she didn't know what to say.

'You don't want me here, do you?' she said at last. 'Any more than you did?'

'No, I don't.'

'You think Johnny's ghost stands between us?'

'Always. I don't understand it, I mean if you'd been left, if your father had died or–'

'It has nothing to do with that. My father was a lovely man, thank you, and he wasn't at all like you. I have a feeling it's that dreadful pull of power–'

'I don't have any of that.'

'If it hadn't been for men like you this would have been a German state by now.'

'You could say the same of any man who did anything towards the war. People contribute what they can.'

'Well then, money, influence, oh ... and a title.'

'Well, yes, of course, how important.'

'So, you're screwing the blonde woman?'

He laughed.

'I am not, as you so delicately put it, screwing the blonde woman.'

'Why not? Her tongue was practically hanging out.'

'Iris...'

'I shall go, then, since you so obviously want me to.'

'It would only make things worse if you stayed,' he said.

'Oh, I doubt things could be any worse.'

'Yes, they could. I could hate you as well.'

'You're so stupid.'

'I know. My mother was always telling me.'

'All I really came for was just to tell you that you were right, that for years and years I pretended I didn't love you because it was the most ridiculous thing. In a way I loved Johnny in spite of you and not the other way round. I just wish I had met you first.'

'You wouldn't have married me.'

'No, but we could have gone to bed in the afternoons and it would have been nice,' she said. 'We could have had one of these rip-roaring affairs and scandalized everybody.'

That made him smile which had been her

intention. After that there was nothing to do but leave. She reached the car and then she called herself names as she started up Ella's little car and tore back down the road towards the city.

The following day was Sunday and Iris lay in bed in case her mother should ask her to go to church, she didn't see how she could face it. When she was quite certain that her mother had left she sauntered down.

Ella and David were playing in the garden with the children and Flo was fussing over the meat on the kitchen stove. Iris was hungry by then. Flo eyed her and when she hovered cut big slices of white bread and dipped them in the fat under the beef. Iris sat at the kitchen table and ate them hot and then she helped Flo to do the vegetables before venturing outside.

It was a bright day. She went and sat under the trees and David joined her there, saying to her, 'I think I've sorted one of your problems.'

'Really?'

'Do you think Wilkie would manage without the shop?'

Iris sat up, shading her eyes from the sunshine which reached through the branches and bright green leaves.

'Why?'

'Well, I've got a house free. She wouldn't

309

have to pay any rent–'

'Wilkie won't take charity.'

'It's a good house, semi-detached in Valley View–'

'But, David, Valley View isn't a foundry house at all. You've been renting it out to old Mrs Coburn forever.'

'She had a heart attack yesterday. I went to see her in hospital and they think she won't last the week.'

'How very considerate of her,' Iris said.

'She is about ninety. She never paid any rent so there's nothing lost. Father would never take it once her husband had died and she's been in there thirty years.'

'It would be wonderful,' Iris said, 'without the rent Wilkie might be able to manage and it has three bedrooms and a garden. I'm going to go and tell Wilkie right now. Can we go and see it?'

David produced the key from his pocket and she snatched it from him, saying only over her shoulder, 'Save me some dinner for later,' before she went.

Mrs Coburn died two days later and Iris couldn't help being pleased. The house was everything that Wilkie had wanted and never thought she would have.

'Your sister-in-law is lucky to have a man like David,' she said, not looking at Iris as they inspected the place for the second time.

'Oh, I don't know,' Iris said, 'he's good but rather dull, don't you think?'

Wilkie turned from gazing around at the ample proportions of the sitting room of her new house and smiled in acknowledgement of Iris's sisterly remark.

'He's very generous. It's a lovely house.'

It was, Iris thought, with a sigh of satisfaction and though she wouldn't have said so she knew David could have asked a good rent for the house though he would not have done so.

Mr and Mrs Turnbull who lived next door and were elderly had never paid rent either. It was their father's gift to the community. Mr Turnbull had been injured in a motor accident years ago. It was understood that he and his wife would live there rent-free until they died.

They were stone houses with big back yards which faced the railway line to the north of the city. The fronts of them had neat gardens. They were solidly built of square stone blocks and compared to the pit cottage where Wilkie and her family were coming from they were luxurious, with a bathroom, separate dining and sitting room and a big kitchen and pantry at the back.

It was even furnished, for the old woman had had nobody to leave anything to and although it was all in need of a good clean the four women were so enthusiastic with their washing, scrubbing and turning out that within a week the little shop at Heath Houses was closed for good, David had sent a van for their belongings and the whole family had moved into town.

Joyce settled the older children into school, Wilkie had a new job at Dryburn Hospital and Iris felt that she and David had done something substantial to help.

Jack had decided to sell the castle. In some moments he believed that it was a brave thing to do and in others he called himself a coward because part of the reason for selling it was because he would have no reason for going to Durham and most of all he would not have to go back into a place where he had memories of Iris with him and worse of her having been there with Johnny and of how she had looked having just got out of his bed. He could never have slept with her there because of it. Every so often he wondered whether if she had come to him at some other place he would have done so.

In London however he thought of Iris, longed for her, cursed that he had left her but did nothing. He had had some semblance of a life before she turned up that last time at the castle and he could not think.

Nan spoiled his concentration further by coming to the office. He barely gazed at her and then did. She looked different. He couldn't think what it was but he got up as she came in, throwing down gloves and handbag, saying in the now confident way she had, 'Are you never coming to see the children?'

'How long has it been?' he said, feeling guilty.

'At least two months. What on earth are you doing? The Second World War is over, you know. Why don't you let somebody else deal with things?'

'Because, unlike the rest of the world, Nan, darling, I am indispensable.'

She rewarded him with a smile and then hesitated.

'Oh dear,' he said, 'you have something unpleasant to tell me.'

'It isn't unpleasant, at least...'

'It isn't something to do with the boys, is it?'

'No, no, at least not directly. It's just that I'm not sure you'll be pleased, you'll try to be, even pretend to be but...' She looked nervously at him.

'Is it something you're pleased about?'

Nan took a short breath and said, 'Sam Eastern has asked me to marry him.'

She was right, it was good news but it was also the end of her being Johnny's widow and though he knew that officially her grieving was long since over marrying again was a sure sign that she was no longer prepared to stay in the role.

'I see.'

She came to him. 'Would you hate it?'

Samuel Eastern was a successful barrister, very respected.

'Do you love him?'

'Yes.'

'Then I'm pleased for you. The boys need a father, Sam is a very good man and I couldn't wish you to go on grieving over Johnny's memory for ever.'

'You'll dance at my wedding with a reasonably light heart?'

'Certainly,' Jack said.

'Then I will tell him yes.'

'You didn't need to ask me.'

'Yes, I did.' She looked at him from clear grey eyes. 'You're the only relative I have since my mother died and you mean a great deal to me and you're the boys' only other blood relative. I don't want to marry a man you dislike or despise so that we don't see you. It's very important to me.'

Jack kissed her.

'I'll be there,' he said.

'Good. I want you to come and stay at the weekend. The boys will be home and I've invited Sam to dinner on Saturday night.'

'Did I tell you I'm selling the castle?' He knew he hadn't told her but he was trying to be casual about it.

'I can't think why you didn't sell it sooner,' she said.

Jack knew why. He remembered the sound of Anna's voice there and of Johnny as a child but now it was sullied by his memories of his guilt over Iris. He would do well to get rid of it.

It appeared to Iris that David had something on his mind. It must be something with regard to work, she decided, because as far as she could judge there was nothing wrong at home and Ella seemed unperturbed so she didn't say anything until they were alone in the sitting room when Lottie had gone out to see some friends and Ella had gone to put Clyde to bed.

'Did you know that Rowarth Castle is up for sale?' David said.

Iris went quite cool. She had told herself that Jack would return to Durham eventually but if he sold the castle he would have no legitimate reason for doing so.

'Well,' she said, 'Ella's always wanted a bigger house.'

'Do you hear anything from Jack?'

Iris took a swig of her gin and tonic and said, 'No.' She reached forward and lifted the lid of the silver cigarette box which had her father's name engraved on it, a gift from some organization he had helped. She offered the box to David and when he took one she took a cigarette herself. He gave her a light, lit his own. They sat back. Ella came in, sighing.

'I could use one of those,' she said.

David gave her a cigarette, poured her a drink. She sat down beside Iris on the sofa.

'Jack is selling the castle,' Iris said, as much to get used to the idea herself as inform Ella.

'I know,' Ella said, 'I just didn't like to tell you. One of my old school friends, Pamela Johnson, knows them in London. Nan is getting married again, some prominent barrister, very important.'

Jealousy consumed Iris to such an extent that she was only amazed she didn't turn into a small heap of ashes where she sat.

'Well, that's it, then,' she said.

'Would you like another drink?' David offered, getting to his feet.

'I would like the biggest gin and tonic in the history of the world,' Iris said.

Iris felt nothing but weariness when she went to bed and a vague feeling against the Fenwicks, father and son. She did not understand what it was like to have a child, to see that child grow up and then die long before his time. No wonder Jack wants to sell the castle, she thought, his memories of Johnny, himself and me must be intolerable. I'll learn to live without him, I'll train to do something, I'll meet somebody new.

The trouble was that she lay awake, remembering the sound of his voice and the way he had sat in the chair and looked down into his drink instead of drinking it as though the effort was too much.

She missed him, as she had always missed him. It was not something she could get used to. Maybe, she thought, I'll go on missing him for the rest of my life. Ever since the day we met I have missed him and in all that time we have seen one another less than half a dozen times and now I may never see him again and there's nothing I can do about it. I've gone to him twice now. He isn't going to come to me, his selling of the castle makes that clear. When he comes back to the North he'll only come to the works on the Tyne. He will never come back to Durham any more.

Nan's dinner was not the intimate occasion Jack had hoped for. The boys were to eat separately though he did get to spend the afternoon with them first. But they were to go to bed early and were most unhappy about it. Jack escaped upstairs with them.

'So what do you think of Mr Eastern?' he said, sitting down on Edward's bed.

'He's all right,' Edward said with fine disregard.

'John?'

His elder grandson shrugged.

'I suppose she may as well marry him as anybody. It isn't as if she's really old like you.'

'True,' Jack said.

'Sorry.'

'No, it's a fact.'

'Mother says you're selling the castle. Why are you doing that?'

'We live in London now.'

Neither of the boys said anything, but they looked at one another.

'Is it a problem?' Jack was amazed. He didn't think either of them cared.

'It was your father's house, wasn't it?' John said.

'Yes, he ... he was very fond of it.'

'And Daddy,' Edward said. 'Daddy liked it too.'

'Yes, he did.'

John looked at him.

'We thought that we would have it.'

'A castle in the middle of nowhere?' Jack said.

'It isn't in the middle of nowhere,' John was defiant. His eyes were lit and defensive. 'We'll have nothing to remember our father by soon. We like London though we're not too keen on school but Durham is home. After Grandma died, Mother sold the house. The way things are going we'll have nothing left there at all. We thought the castle was for us.'

Jack was astonished. He had had no idea they felt like that and he cursed himself for his insensitivity.

'Do you have a buyer for it?' John said.

'Not yet.'

Edward came forward and deposited several hot pennies into Jack's hand.

'I was saving this for a bike–'

'Don't be silly, Ned,' his brother said.

'It's only a deposit,' Ned insisted.

'It costs thousands of pounds to buy a castle, you can't do it with a few pennies.'

'I will give you the rest later,' Edward said, with dignity. 'In the meanwhile you can't sell it because you have my deposit.'

'Ned–'

'No, it's all right,' Jack said. 'Do you have money for your deposit?'

'I have six pounds in my bank account.'

'That should do,' Jack said.

John stared at him.

'You'll sell it to us, then?'

'I will,' Jack said.

'Does that mean we can go home sometimes?' John said eagerly. 'Next holiday? Will you take us?'

'We'll go for Christmas. It usually snows in Durham at Christmas.'

'Mummy can come as well, can't she?' Edward said.

'And Sam.'

'You call him by his name?' Jack asked.

Edward raised his eyes.

'Well, Uncle Sam sounds stupid and we can't call him Daddy, can we?'

'Not yet anyhow,' John said tactfully.

Jack went slowly downstairs and into the dining room. Half a dozen people had arrived. It made him wish he could hide upstairs and play draughts with the boys. He went slowly into a roomful of people. He knew Sam Eastern, he didn't know any of the others. Jack shook his hand, congratulated him and Sam said, like a schoolboy,

'I do hope you don't mind. Perhaps I should have asked you–'

'Of course not,' Jack said.

'But Nan said that she was sure you would be glad for us.'

'I am glad for you.'

It was the first time he had felt old, John was right. He was seated between two beautiful young women who listened intently to whatever he said and asked intelligent questions about his business. Jack longed for Iris, being rude and irrelevant.

He couldn't eat. Everything was tasteless. He didn't like to drink because he was afraid it would make his mood worse. The evening, he was afraid, would never end. His only relief was that he had refused Nan's invitation to stay.

'The boys will miss you,' she said as she walked him out into the hall when he left, 'stay and we'll have a proper old-fashioned Sunday.'

Jack thought that spending Sunday with the man who was about to take his son's place was too difficult at this point. He would do it later. He pleaded work.

'I want you and Sam and the boys to come to Durham for Christmas,' he told her.

She frowned.

'I thought you were selling up.'

'I'm keeping the castle for the boys.'

'They always liked it so much. Sam and I are planning to be married in October so Christmas in the North would be perfect. They do miss it, you know.'

'I wish you'd told me.'

'I didn't like to, considering everything. You must have many memories in that place. I thought perhaps you were selling it because of them.'

'I changed my mind.'

'Well, then,' she said, 'we'll come and we'll have a party and invite everybody and have dancing and music and a band. I miss it too. I miss my mother and my father and all the things that Durham does that nowhere else does for people who were born there. It will probably snow, it always does,' she said, beaming and she kissed him.

Jack went home to the cool of his house, to the silence. When he got there he poured himself a very large Scotch and sat looking over his garden and wondering whether Iris had heard of his decision to sell the castle.

He pictured her coming to London and shouting at him. She wouldn't of course. She had no right to do so, he had not allowed her any. He thought of her braving him at the castle twice. No other woman would have done it, perhaps nobody would have cared as she did.

He pictured her there and it was not as Johnny's lover, not wearing Johnny's shirt and standing by the dining-room doors, he saw her in the doorway the last time they had met, he thought of her upturned nose, her green eyes, her out-of-control mouth and he wished more than he had ever wished anything in his life that he had kissed her, that he had taken her into his arms and told her that he would never let her go, that they would live at the castle forever and that the memories of Johnny being there hurt him no more than the memories of Anna and of their life together and of his parents dying there.

The castle was part of them. How could he ever have thought otherwise? The boys were right. Johnny's sons would have the castle in time, they had not expected anything for nothing, they had bought it, a proper deal, a sale, for the extravagant price of six pounds and seven pence. It was worth every penny, he thought.

Wilkie was surprised to hear a banging on the front door mid-evening. Iris always came round the back and she was their only regular visitor apart from Mrs Turnbull who had baked them a coffee cake when they moved in and confided to Wilkie, who apologized in case the noise of the children should make it through the walls, that she was glad of it, things had been quiet around here for far too long.

Wilkie was working at the hospital and glad that Iris kept coming to help since her mother tired quickly and even though the elder children were at school most of the time there was still a great deal of work to do.

Wilkie opened the front door. To her surprise George stood there.

'I would like to see Joyce,' he said.

'I don't think she wants to see you.'

Joyce, curious and perhaps hearing his voice, came through into the hall.

'George,' she said.

'May I come inside?'

'You can say what you have to say from right there,' Wilkie said.

'I want you to come home.'

'He's drunk,' Wilkie said.

'Has the bishop been at you about us again?' Joyce said.

'It isn't that. I miss you and I miss the

children and I'm sorry for the way that I behaved. If you come back I'll try to make things better for us.'

The second boy, Thomas, followed his mother into the hall. He had always been George's favourite child.

'Daddy,' he said.

'Hello, Tom, how are you?'

'You'd better come in,' Wilkie allowed.

George gazed around him.

'You've fallen on your feet here,' he said.

'No thanks to you,' Wilkie said, unforgiving. 'David Black owns the house. We have it from him rent-free, he's such a good man.'

'The Blacks are all good people, Iris excepted, of course.'

'She's been very kind to us,' Wilkie said.

Matthew stared when George walked into the sitting room.

'What does he want? We're not going back, we're never going back.'

'It's all right, Matt,' Joyce assured him, 'your father is just visiting us.'

Wilkie made tea. Her mother was upstairs, lying down. She had done the ironing that day and probably a great many other things she had omitted to tell Wilkie about. Wilkie hoped if she was awake that she would know it was George and stay put.

George would obviously have been glad of a little privacy but he didn't get any. Three of the children were in the sitting room and

Wiikie was not about to tell him he could talk to Joyce in the dining room or anywhere else that would be private. She didn't trust him.

'I would like us to try again,' he said.

'I'm not going back,' Matt said.

George looked at him.

'Aren't people allowed second chances?' he said.

'You didn't give Mam even a first chance,' Matt said bitterly. 'Because of me. Because you think that I was somebody else's.'

'Matt–' Joyce said.

'It's true,' Matthew said. 'I heard you talking about it, that I didn't belong, that George here–' it was the biggest insult the lad could think of, to call his father by his first name, Wilkie could see. She didn't know what to do or say, this was outside her experience – 'was not my dad. Well, I'm glad he's not my dad because anybody less like me isn't possible and I'm not going back there, I'm going to stay here with my granny and Auntie Wilkie and nothing anybody can say or do will make any difference,' and he ran out of the room, out of the back door. Wilkie heard it clash.

He was, she thought, a very intelligent boy, so he couldn't possibly be George's son, but then that would rule out Melvyn as well.

The other children sat still and nobody spoke.

'Please come back,' George said to Joyce. She looked at her sister.

'It's up to you,' Wilkie said, 'if things go wrong again you can always come here. Why don't you two go for a walk and I'll look after the bairns and you can see what you decide, but mind you, you're not making Matt go. He stays here with us.'

Joyce and George went out the front door and the atmosphere eased. Bess came down the stairs almost immediately. The two middle children were sitting on the sofa together, the smallest child slept on upstairs.

'You heard that, presumably?' Wilkie said, turning from the stove where she was making jam tarts for tea. The smell was wonderful, she had always liked it, the sweet sticky combination of pastry, raspberries and sugar.

'She could give it another try,' her mother said wearily. 'You and Matt and I would manage. I'm happy for you to go on working at the hospital as long as you want to. This place is lovely and I like having Matt here.'

Wilkie smiled at her and nodded and then she took the tray from the oven and shouted so that the children could hear, 'Who's for jam tarts?' and they ran through into the kitchen.

Iris didn't know what to do. It seemed to her that Joyce and Wilkie didn't really need her any more. She could go back to nursing of course but things had moved on so much and she didn't want to. Neither did she want to do secretarial work, George had cured her of that.

She did shopping for Ella, she tried to help around the house but Flo eyed her suspiciously so she had taken to going for a walk in the afternoons just to get away from everybody else. She would walk the towpaths and think about Jack and wonder whether he had sold the castle and if they would ever meet again which seemed most unlikely and filled her with a fear of the future, of getting older by herself, of always being 'Miss Black', of withering away.

The autumn was lovely in the town and she could admire the leaves which fell from the trees on to the river path below the cathedral and she thought of Christmas to come with a sinking heart.

She would not be alone, of course, she would have all the family around her and Clyde and Susan were of an age where Christmas was a pleasure but they were not hers. She was beginning to have to accustom herself to the idea that she would never have any children, that she would remain Auntie Iris.

It was late afternoon, the middle of October, and it was almost dark. She made her way as she must back to the house where she had no place but where Ella and David were making her life as easy as they could. She should not resent them, her fate was not their fault, it was perhaps not anybody's fault.

She walked up the path towards the drive and as she turned in she halted. A cream car was sitting in front of the house. It was not one of theirs, and it was not belonging to anybody local that she knew. It was in fact, she drew nearer, yes, it was Jack Fenwick's Daimler.

Iris took several deep breaths before she opened the door. She would not hope for anything good, she just hoped nothing dreadful had happened to bring him home.

Ella came into the hall as Iris opened the front door.

'There you are,' she said, voice full of relief. 'Jack Fenwick is here.'

'Yes, I saw the car,' Iris said with a backward glance towards the cream Daimler gleaming in the last of the sunlight. 'What does he want?'

'How on earth should I know?' Ella whispered. 'I've been trying to make conversation with him for the last hour. I told him you wouldn't be back for a while but he insisted on waiting.'

Iris walked slowly into the sitting room. Jack was standing by the window, looking out over the lawns which were covered in leaves, brown, gold, lime and lemon coloured.

'Taking an interest in gardening, are you?' Iris greeted him. 'You could start by raking the leaves off the lawn. They ruin the grass, you know.'

He turned, smiling.

'Hello, Iris,' he said.

'You never buy a new car, do you? Can't you afford it?'

'Actually it belongs to the company. I don't own a car.'

'Otherwise you'd drive something really modest. I can imagine. And to what do we owe this pleasure? I thought you'd sold up and left.'

'I changed my mind.'

'Gosh, London will be the poorer for it.'

'Nan is getting married again.'

'We heard. Some posh barrister. Good for her.'

'And the boys wanted to come to Durham for Christmas.'

'Sounds lovely,' Iris said. 'Aren't you a little early for that?'

He hesitated. Iris waited.

'I don't know how to say this,' he said.

'Well, do your best,' she encouraged him. 'I haven't had any tea yet and do sit down, you're making me nervous.'

Jack laughed uneasily and eyed her.

'It isn't something awful, is it?' Iris said, unable to wait any longer.

'I love you, Iris.'

She laughed. It sort of burst out of her without her being able to stop it.

'I suppose some people would consider that awful.'

'Is it?' he said.

'I know you do. I never doubted it, at least not since the first time I ventured to the castle and we agreed about these things. Going to your place isn't something I think I ever want to do again, not after the last twice when I made a fool of myself.'

Iris had the horrible feeling that she was about to faint and it was a curiously freeing sensation and then she breathed consciously for a few moments and waited for Jack to go on.

'I know I haven't...' he said and then stopped. 'I want you to marry me.'

Iris considered the only other proposal she had had and it was Johnny in this very room. That didn't make things any easier and yet she knew such joy in the seconds that followed that she was convinced even further that she would faint and was obliged to sit down quite suddenly, almost missing the easy chair which had been her father's favourite.

'Oh God,' she said.

'I'm sorry, I...' he said. 'I didn't know how else to say it. I did consider ways of doing it but I hadn't thought you would be out when

I got here and I spent ages talking to your sister-in-law about the roses since I couldn't remember the names of her children and it seemed so rude and ... by the time you got here I lost my nerve and anything eloquent I might have thought of.'

'I don't remember you ever being eloquent,' she said.

'No, well. I'm sorry, especially after last time.'

'What made you change your mind?'

'I didn't change my mind, it was just that ... when I went to see the boys they talked about the castle and how they loved it and how this was home and how many happy memories they had of – of being there and the things they remember about their father. I didn't want to take that away from them. They wanted to come home for Christmas and so do I. I want to come home to you.'

'Now you're in danger of being eloquent,' she said, 'stop it at once or I shall cry. I don't see how I can marry you really, Jack.'

A shadow fell over his face.

'It would be so awful for my enemies to have to address me as Lady Fenwick. You do see the problem.' She got up, tripped over the fireside rug, cast herself upon him and said, 'I love you to pieces, idiot, and of course I will marry you.'

'Oh, hell, I'm so pleased. Thank God,' and his arms closed around her.

Ella was standing in the hall when David got back from work.

'What are you doing?' he asked.

'Shush a minute.' She held up a delaying hand. David closed the outside door softly.

'What is going on?' he whispered.

'Jack Fenwick is proposing to Iris.'

'Holy hell, is he really?'

'Yes, David, yes, he really is.'

'And what is she saying?'

'I don't know. I can't hear now.'

They both listened close to the sitting-room door and then they heard laughter and presently Iris came out of the room, her face transformed.

'Ella,' she said, 'would you like to be my matron of honour?'

Ella squealed. Jack Fenwick came to the door and his expression, David thought, could only be described as sheepish.

'You don't mind, do you?' he said.

David shook his hand.

'Welcome to the family,' he said.

'I want a big wedding,' Iris said, 'nothing modest. I want the biggest wedding in the whole world and I want a diamond, a great big diamond.'

'Only one?' Jack said.

Books used for Reference and Information

Andrews, Lucilla. *No Time for Romance,* Corgi, 2007

Bowden, Jean. *Grey Touched with Scarlet,* Hale, 1959

Eldridge, Jim. *Desert Danger,* My Story Series, Scholastic, 2005

McBryde, Brenda. *A Nurse's War,* Cakebreads Publications, (revised), 1993

McBryde, Brenda. *Quiet Heroines: Nurse of the Second World War,* Chatto & Windus, 1985

Hay, Ian. *One Hundred Years of Army Nursing,* Cassell, 1953

Peacock, John. *The 1950s (Fashion Sourcebooks),* Thames & Hudson, 1997

Peacock, John. *The 1940s (Fashion Sourcebooks),* Thames & Hudson, 1998

Piggott, Juliet. *Queen Alexandra's Royal Army Nursing Corps,* Famous Regiments Series, Leo Cooper, 1975

Scoullar, Lieutenant-Colonel J.L. *Battle for Egypt,* War History Branch, Wellington, 1955

Starns, Penny. *Nurses at War: Women on the Frontline 1939–45*, Sutton Publishing, 2000

Taylor, Eric. *Front-Line Nurse: British Nurses in World War II*, Robert Hale, 1997

The publishers hope that this book has given you enjoyable reading. Large Print Books are especially designed to be as easy to see and hold as possible. If you wish a complete list of our books please ask at your local library or write directly to:

Magna Large Print Books
Magna House, Long Preston,
Skipton, North Yorkshire.
BD23 4ND

This Large Print Book, for people
who cannot read normal print,
is published under the auspices of

THE ULVERSCROFT FOUNDATION